MILFORD COAL & ICE

Book 2 in the Gwendolyn Strong Small Town Cozy Mystery Series

J A HODA

Copyright © 2022 by J A hoda

All rights reserved.

No part of this book may be reproduced in any form or by any electronic or mechanical means, including information storage and retrieval systems, without written permission from the author, except for the use of brief quotations in a book review. All character are purely fictional. Any resemblance to living persons is purely coincidental

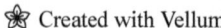 Created with Vellum

CHAPTER ONE

"Look out!" I yell. The kid pulling his sled up the hill backwards is not looking where he's going. He turns, his eyes wide. Like a matador, he sidesteps us in the nick of time.

Our toboggan flies down the hill past him. My youngest granddaughter, April, shrieks joyfully as snowflakes kiss her face. The wooden slats undulate under our bums as we skim over the snow.

This is the best place for sledding in all the county. The Bloodstone family mansion reopened as Milford's Commerce and Industry museum two years ago. The snow-covered lawn steeply drops towards the state highway, and the river beyond is perfect for a winter day's outing with my adorable grandchildren.

My son, Wesley, and my oldest grandson, Caleb, are trying their best to catch us. The race is on. My daughter, Erin, and her middle child, Jesse, are laughing too hard to steer straight, although steering a toboggan is an interesting proposition at any speed.

We arrived this morning bundled up complete with mittens and scarves as the first intrepid group to test a foot of virgin snow, and we've been up and down the slope dozens of times before lunch, each time going faster and faster as more arriving sleds pack the snow into a sheen of white ice.

I took one look at the weather forecast the night before and gleefully planned for a snow day.

For thirty-five years, I was Gwendolyn Strong, kindergarten teacher. That was until the Board of Education shuttered Milford Elementary this past fall. My child-like excitement always ramps up when I hear the school-closing announcement on the radio.

At dawn, I looked out the window to the blanket of white fluffy snow. I excitedly talked my unmarried son into taking a personal day from his work as an accountant to join me, Erin, and my three grandkiddies for a morning of tobogganing. My husband, Ken, had pulled three curve-nosed wooden toboggans from the rafters of our garage, and we waxed them the night before in anticipation of our snow day.

Erin met us in the mansion parking lot. Food trucks with their generators humming had already arrived, preparing the day's sustenance for the anticipated horde of sledders.

"Whee!" April and I yell together as we cross the finish line five yards ahead of Wes and Caleb. I dig my heels into the snow, and we come to a stop twenty yards before the snow disappears into rows of trees and laurel along the state highway.

Our breathless clan makes it down the hill safely. My fifty-seven-year-old legs are in better shape than both of my sedentary kids. I hoist April on my shoulders, and we make our way up the long, steep hill to the promise of tomato soup, grilled cheese sandwiches, roasted chestnuts, and hot chocolate.

Yoga and walking this autumn turned what could have been a depressing slide into voluntary retirement into an active lifestyle to go with my unexpected encore as an amateur sleuth.

Wesley calls me a shameless shamus. Erin tells any curious townspeople that everything her mother learned about solving mysteries, she learned in kindergarten. My daughter homeschools her oldest two by day, but she also works as a civilian contractor for the FBI at night, gathering intelligence from select social media sites. She has an encyclopedic knowledge of how all the cable TV true crime cases are solved, but we don't share any of these little tidbits with the public.

I, on the other hand, have been told that I am the one with an observant eye and who has a solid grasp of human nature. There must be something about teaching kindergarteners for thirty-five years, I guess. These gifts allow me to look at things a bit differently and has led to some interesting conclusions. My family is split on the idea of a wife and mother chasing down clues in her spare time. The men would like me to pursue other interests. Erin is my biggest fan and confidant.

Abe Schatz and Emelina Bidwell at the yoga studio refuse to allow me to slink off into the sunset. They tell me often I have something special, and if I did not to share it with the good folks of Milford, it would be a damn shame. They use more colorful language, though.

April and I are first up the hill, and we look back at the laggards. "C'mon, you slow pokes!" I yell.

"C'mon, you slow pokes!" April mimics me mischievously. We make a great pair.

As if it was planned, my better half arrives with his truck. Ken is joining us for lunch. We stand in line with the rest of our clan after throwing the toboggans into his truck bed.

"How was your morning, dear?" I ask.

Ken is Milford's most sought-after home remodeler, handyman, and woodworker. He restores homes throughout the area. This week he started working on a mansion built before the Civil War. The latest owner, a retired pulmonologist from the city, wants to return it to its antebellum condition and also update it with solar on the back roof to power the electric heat, air conditioning, and a hot tub tucked away in a backyard gazebo.

"I feel like a ping-pong ball getting paddled between the building inspector wanting things brought up to code and the historical commission wanting to preserve the building to its original condition."

"That is a definition of being stuck between a rock and a hard place," I say.

"A prior owner walled off the coal furnace and replaced it with oil years ago. You would think that I am doing an archaeological dig when I go to knock down the studs and paneling to remove the coal furnace. They both want to be there this afternoon when I do it."

"Why?"

"Environmental hazards. They are worried about asbestos."

"Everybody has to have a say." Secretly, I am glad they are worried about asbestos. It's my husband's lungs at risk here, but I won't say it out loud as long as the professionals are doing so.

"I know, I know, but it just slows my work down. I'm already starting to get backed up," he says.

Usually, wintertime is his slow season, but he has just finished a big project for Abe and was handed this one on top of all the handyman requests he gets. He's busier than I've seen him in a long time. He feels like he can't turn down any work after I volunteered to take a lay-off. The union is haggling with the school board on how to calculate my sick time and vacation time lump sum payouts, so I will exhaust the unemployment benefits until I take my pension.

We've gone over the numbers a few times. We have no big expenses; everything is paid off. The house we are rehabbing now, which we live in, was bought with cash. We will be able to flip it for a tidy profit in the spring. Ken is not showing any signs of slowing down and loves what he does. I can't get the man to take a vacation; he just wants to get up in the morning and work with his hands all day. It keeps him physically fit and mentally sharp. Who am I to argue with that?

The food trucks are doing a booming business, making me think about another possibility that is warming in my oven of opportunities. Centenarian Emelina Bidwell has decided to use her formidable baking skills to begin selling her prized chocolate chip cookies and other goodies. She wants somebody to pass the recipes onto. That somebody is me. Ken upgraded the kitchen at the yoga studio to commercial grade, and the final inspections are completed. Her food license is awaiting Board of Health approval at the next town meeting. She is going to bring a dozen of her finest to set next to the coffee urn, but only after the meeting starts. The board will have to smell them as they plod through the agenda.

We find a picnic table and brush off all the snow. A cornucopia of winter treats is passed around, family style. My grandkids are well-behaved, especially as they are outnumbered by the adults, and everyone has a huge appetite. Everything that is supposed to be warm is warm, and the tomato soup and hot chocolate are as you would expect on a cold wintry day. The snow has stopped and the sun gleams through icicles hanging from the rows of maples and elms that ring the mansion's rear parking lot. A Norman Rockwell painting or two comes to mind as I stare with joy at my family gathered on this impromptu feast day. I know that not every family is blessed with harmony and closeness. Tragedy can happen in a blink of an eye. I am grateful for all that I have.

~

I offer nine-year-old Caleb twenty dollars to shovel our driveway upon our return to the house. His eyes are like saucers at the thought of making so much money. Wesley agrees to supervise while the girls go about the serious work of building snow pals. Inclusive language is not new to me, but Erin and the grandchildren are much more practiced. We settle on making nameless big, medium, and little ones.

We must keep our little doggie from peeing on them, though. Ken and I rescued Billy from the shelter just before Thanksgiving. He is part beagle and part cocker spaniel and is just over a year old. Normally on a leash with me on my jaunts around town, he frolics in the snow between us on the lawn and the boys on the driveway. He has learned the words "stay" and "come"—he won't run away.

"Mrs. Pearce gave you quite the gift, Mom," Erin says. "Do you have any plans for using it?"

My daughter reminds me about how Billy and I recovered her prized award-winning Australian Cattle Dog. The money is a sizable sum more than the posted reward, but a lot less than the ransom.

I offer her a wide smile. "Don't forget she gave a hefty contribution to the animal shelter," I say.

"An endowment fund in your name," Erin replies proudly with a knowing grin.

She lifts a basketball-sized ball of snow onto the biggest one. Six-year-old Jesse finds a suitable carrot from my pantry and coal from our tool shed to decorate the face.

"CrimeCon is in Vegas this year, Mom," Erin says excitedly. "We could do another girl's weekend. I could write it off on my taxes to offset the money I make from the FBI." She is talking about an annual gathering of all things true crime. Thousands of aficionados camp out for a long weekend at a destination hotel to gorge on unsolved mysteries. Guest speakers and cable stars of the crime networks are the main draw, but the convention hall is also filled with rows of podcasters who have changed how cold cases get solved by crowdsourcing them. Erin and I know a little about podcasters crowdsourcing investigations into cold cases.

Remembering our trip to New Haven the year before, I say, "We do learn a great deal at those things, honey." We help the girls roll up the base for the middle snow pal.

"Besides, learning new skills for your new career will come in handy."

"New career? I am not sure you could call it a new career."

"You told me that you don't need to earn an income. You can do anything your heart desires."

We deadlift a large round mound of snow onto the base, while the girls start forming the head of the medium one. "I know, but I have another opportunity to explore. Emelina Bidwell wants to start selling her cookies and other baked goodies."

Erin says, "See, you are never too late in life to start a business."

"And she wants to teach me her recipes."

"I'd say she is a pretty good teacher, Mom. She continued mentoring you after she taught kindergarten for forty years."

"I think there is more to it than that. She never married or had kids. I might be the closest thing to family for her."

"You're a pretty good baker yourself. You taught me everything I know."

I close my eyes to savor the memories of Erin standing on a stool and pouring batter on the cookie sheets next to me in the kitchen. Smells of cinnamon and molasses come flooding back. "I know, but people fight over her chocolate chip cookies. Your dad redid her bathroom just for a large batch. He didn't even share one with me and kept them hidden until they were all gone."

Erin laughs. "I get it. But is she really serious about it?"

"Dad built a baker's kitchen at the yoga studio for her, and she is getting her food license at the next board meeting."

"I guess there are no exemptions for one-hundred-year-olds, huh?"

"Not when it comes to collecting license fees. Just ask your dad every time he has to renew his."

"So, what are you thinking, Mom?" she asks.

"I think it would be fun to learn Emelina's secrets. The money, if we made any, would be like a paying hobby for me."

"Not a side hustle?"

I shake my head. "I don't know, that is up to Emelina. I am just the trainee."

Caleb and Wesley are done shoveling the driveway. One gets paid, the other will get a back rub on the floor in front of the fireplace. The girls have already moved onto baby snow pal.

"Why can't you do both?" Erin askes me.

"I don't know, Milford is a small town. How much mystery can there be?"

"Bill Spencer, the private investigator from the Stillman case, would hire you in a New York minute. You know he would put you on his license. All you have to do is say yes."

I blush, even though my cheeks are numb from the cold. "I know, but I'm not sure I want to look into that for now."

The mid-afternoon sun disappears behind dark clouds. Another round of snow is forecast for later this evening.

The girls make quick work. The adults fawn over their snow sculptures. We take photos of them with their creations, then they run into the house to get warm just as Ken pulls into the shoveled driveway.

"Caleb and Wesley took care of it for you," I say, pointing of their effort. Ken gets out of his truck and doesn't look where I am pointing or say anything in reply. Something's not right. My husband appears agitated. He is not connecting with me and has a faraway stare. Ken is pale, sweating, and swallowing repeatedly. Something is definitely wrong. Is he about to have a heart attack?

"Why are you home so early? Everything go alright with the inspection?" I try to act calm, keeping concern out of my voice.

Erin closes in next to me and glances at me with a worried look on her face and then stares at him. "Daddy?"

He closes his eyes, sways on unsteady feet, and grabs the trucks door frame. "We found a dead body."

CHAPTER TWO

The grandchildren are happily watching TV and playing games on an iPad in the den. Billy scampers in to be with April. The adults wait for Ken to speak as he stares at the fire crackling in the fireplace. I hand him a mug of coffee. We will stay with him until he's ready to speak. He sips and sighs. Closing his eyes, he is either shutting out the discovery in his mind or recalling it.

"I guess there is a first time for everything," he starts. "Over the years, I have gone into basements or attics and found things left by the prior owners. I always ask permission of the new owners if they will let me keep anything of value as I sort through the junk before carting it off."

"I remember you found an entire collection of Hardy Boys and Nancy Drew mysteries," Erin says. "They were dusty, but in mint condition. When my kiddos are old enough, I will bring them out of storage."

I know Ken is physically safe now, but I've never seen him this circumspect. I think it was the surprise as much as anything that has him searching for words.

"Didn't we get one of our toboggans that way, Dad?" Wesley asks.

"Yes, it was from Mrs. Penn's garage," he says while staring at the flames. He sips and sighs.

Found treasure, we called it. Recipe books with twenty-dollar bills stuck between the pages. Family bibles which Ken took to the historical society, as the birth, death, and marriage information of generations were better than what you would find on the genealogy databases. Stock certificates stuffed in old *Life* magazines. Martin acoustic guitars with a string missing. Forgotten treasure.

The porcelain baby dolls and wedding dresses went to Goodwill. A German luger, swords, knives, and other war memorabilia, my husband sold on consignment at Big Ed's pawn shop. Some days, Ken would come home from work with a big smile on his face. After dinner he'd make a big deal of his discoveries, setting them among the dessert plates.

Now, he puts down the mug on the coffee table and nervously rubs his hands. "I busted open the paneling. It was hung on two by fours. No insulation. Really cheap. Very easy to dismantle, as it was not a load-bearing wall. The casement windows supplied enough lighting to see the coal furnace, bin, and chute. After we agreed the contraption and duct work were built before anybody even thought of using asbestos, we all breathed in deeply. It sat untouched for decades. The grate for the furnace was rusted shut, a coal shovel next to it. The bin still had coal in it, and next to it sat a steamer trunk standing on its end."

He seemed hesitant in what to say next. My husband pulled his cellphone from his pocket and began fiddling with it. "I started to move it and the leather straps holding it together disintegrated. Everything spilled out onto the floor, kicking up the coal dust. We waited until the dust settled, then this is what we saw."

He holds out his phone for Erin. "The new owner asked me to

snap a few pictures. He didn't want to believe me until I showed him."

She examines it closely and enlarges the photo. My husband, freed from the burden, reaches for his coffee, sipping it slowly while staring into the flames.

"What do you see, honey?" I ask her.

"A woman's skeleton."

Wesley, my youngest, gasps, "Oh my God!"

"Yeah," Ken says, "it fell out right at our feet. The building inspector had a similar reaction before he threw up. I wasn't feeling much better after he did that. My stomach lurched a few times."

"That explains why you were white as a ghost when you came home," I say. Wes and I don't move to grab the phone from Erin. She knows Wes and will show me when she is good and ready.

"Anything in the trunk to identify her?"

"You mean like a note pinned to her dress?" He doesn't look at me when he delivers that retort.

Ken doesn't usually smart-ass me or the kids, so I understand it's because he's upset. "We all backed off and called 911, then we waited upstairs until Barney came. We called the owner again. A skeleton found in a trunk in a basement was not what he was expecting. After he talked to Barney, I packed up my tools and bolted."

"Are they treating like a crime scene?" she asks.

He shrugs. "I wouldn't have a clue."

Barney is Officer Williams, one of two full-time police officers on the Milford Police Department. He is the daytime weekday officer. Nights, holidays, and weekends are handled by the other officer and two part-timers.

My phone buzzes in my pocket. Erin text me the photos Ken had taken.

The trunk had been lined with crumbling newspaper and

drapes. A tattered coat and dress hung on the skeleton's bones. A patent leather shoe clung stubbornly to the bones of the right foot. An interesting piece of jewelry was draped across the top of the spinal column below the skull.

"Is that a wedding ring?" I ask her, looking at the left hand folded across the right in front of her chest.

"I wouldn't doubt it," Erin replies.

"It might hold an inscription of the marriage date and their initials," I say knowingly from my own wedding band.

"Jesus Christ. What's the matter with you two?" Ken pounds his mug on the table, then gets up. I hear the front door open, then slam shut.

"I'll talk to him, Mom," Erin says as she hands the phone to Wes and chases after her father.

He's not sure that he wants to look, but he refreshes the screen and I get to see my husband's initial reaction to the scene though my son. "How can you both be so—" he is struggling for the right words "—freaking *clinical*." He puts the phone face down on the coffee table next to his father's mug, probably wishing he never saw the image.

I think back to a time when he and Erin were young. The four of us were going somewhere and we came across a deer hit by a car. The poor thing was splayed across our travel lane, barely alive, blood everywhere. Wesley cried the whole way home and was inconsolable. His nightmares didn't go away for months.

Freaking clinical. "That's a pretty fair assessment, dear." Why didn't Erin and I get upset? Instead, we are already looking for clues of the identity of the woman stuffed in a trunk and hidden behind a wall. Why *are* we so freaking clinical? It's a fair question. Will looking at skeletons and dead bodies come back to haunt us someday?

For thirty-five years, I wiped runny noses, blew kisses on skinned knees, and hugged hurting five-year-olds, all the while trying to teach them how to share, be nice, work together, and have a curious mind. I never gave two thoughts about TV whodunits. My bedstand reading consisted of self-improvement, biographies of inspirational people, and post-apocalyptic dystopian thrillers.

But when Erin and I went to New Haven, Connecticut last year for the true crime symposium, something clicked in me, and all those years of being in the moment of wiping runny noses and mindfully clapping erasers helped me discover this so-called higher purpose. Erin will eventually become an investigator, I am sure. She is committed to both homeschooling my adorable grandchildren and her part-time gig with the FBI for now. I look at her and know that Nancy Drew grew up. But what about me, a bi-racial retired kindergarten teacher? An hour ago, I had complained that small town Milford didn't have any mysteries.

I look at my son and say, "In the proverbial lifeboat, there are those who row the boat and those who just drink the water. I don't have a choice, Wes. I must ask who is she? How did she get there? What is her story? If I don't, I am just drinking the water. Do you understand, honey?"

CHAPTER THREE

Breathing in during morning meditation at the yoga studio, I think about how frosty it was in my bed last night. I breathe out and notice how lonely my skin feels without Ken's caresses and hugs this morning. Neither of us must wake up to an alarm clock anymore. It makes for some interesting ways to start our day. Not today, however.

I breathe in slowly to the memory of him in the shower, then the sound of the coffee pot dripping out his coffee. I breathe out to the only mumbled words my honey had for me this morning, something about getting breakfast at the diner. I expand my abdomen with air as I remember holding the coffee carafe upside down with the realization that he only made enough wake-up juice for himself. I expel the air from my abdomen through my nose softly as I purse my unkissed lips. He has never left the house without kissing me before this morning. He didn't come home last night until after I was in bed. Where he went and what he ate for dinner is a mystery to me as I get into my thoughts and stop concentrating on my breath. It's no use meditating this morning. Nirvana will have to wait another day.

As the saying stenciled on the baby bib laments, "Spit

Happens." Ken and I had our spats over the years. Mostly it had to do with money or how to handle Erin, who was a handful as a child. Her ADHD was diagnosed early, but we chose not to treat her with medication. It made for a "fun" time at home and at school, especially with some of my peers, who would have liked to have drugged all their pupils into a zombie-like state. Borrowing images from the submarine movies, I can't think of a time when he went silent running on me. He must be really upset.

Erin thinks he was expecting comfort and sympathy to his discovering that sack of bones that spilled out of the trunk. She and I put on our Sherlock Holmes caps instead. Then there is that male macho thing about not expecting comfort and sympathy from your wife or daughter. So he's also angry at himself. The last thing she said to me last night before I told her to love and hug my grandchildren was that he was in a very emotional state and we were not. I told her that Wesley said we were freaking clinical. She laughed but agreed that we didn't make the right sounds when Ken showed us his phone. He saw his dynamic duo at work and felt we treated him like a witness and not as a loved one.

I don't have to wonder why my guy is in knots. I unfold my legs, get to my unsteady feet, and reach for my bolster to place on the shelf. In the few minutes between meditation and yoga, the regulars huddle to talk about the grisly find. In a small town, one doesn't have to wait for the morning news on TV or the newspaper thrown onto the driveway to get the top story.

The two town officials on the scene tell their family and closest friends. The State Police crime scene techs talk about the ghastly finding while passing the gravy and mashed potatoes around the dinner table. I don't have to tell you about social media. Connections are made to who owned the house when the partition went up, who may have installed the oil furnace and hot water radiators, who delivered the oil, and so on. I'm gathering intelligence as fast as you can say "plank pose." Abe sits back and pretends to busy himself with his music for today's session. Emelina is circling our group as a few of the less shy yogis ask me if Ken shared his photos with me and if could I show them. So they already knew about the photos. I tell them it is not my place to do so, and they must ask him.

We take our place on our mats as class begins. I mull over all the information Milford's denizens came up with overnight. There is a lot of grain to separate from chaff as I half-listen to Abe. We move through the sun salutations, then into the seated poses and finally Shavasana. I refuse to call it corpse pose since the Stillman case, another murder case I helped solve a few months ago. I don't fall asleep this time, but I am calmer than when we started. My little pooch Billy loves helping the yogis with their poses, and he is snoozing on his own mat in a ray of sunshine in the middle of the floor.

I know I must apologize to Ken and let him know that I will be more understanding the next time a skeleton falls out of a trunk he is holding on to.

Emelina asks, "Can I see you in the kitchen, Gwen?"

We cross into the brand-new space. Two sinks, three ovens, a new stove, a humongous freezer, and an oversized refrigerator are all laid out for easy access. Their gleaming surfaces scream "brand new.". Abe didn't go cheap on the built-in cabinetry or electrical outlets either.

"Can you go with me this afternoon to meet Benjamin over at the Chamber?" she asks.

"Sure, what is going on?"

"The Chamber is throwing a President's day bash for their membership drive and want us to cater the desserts."

"Our first paying customer," I exclaim.

"We have to give him a quote, and I am bringing a sample of some of the things we can do. I spent half the night in my home kitchen getting all the goodies together."

"Have you thought of a name for the business yet, Em?" I ask.

"Why do you ask?"

"We could have business cards printed up for people to take home. All the Chamber members and their spouses will be there. It would be like a launch party for you."

"I hadn't thought of it like that," she says. "Everyone already knows me, and I am still listed in the telephone book."

True, I thought. I've known her all my years in Milford. Who doesn't? "A business name would let everyone know you are doing more than just charity events."

"How exciting, Gwen. I will meditate on that idea." She pauses, then looks over my shoulder to see that no one is approaching. "There is one other thing. Do I understand it correctly that Ken found a skeleton of a woman that had been stuffed in a steamer trunk?"

I nod my head.

"People are saying that they think the basement where he found her was partitioned about fifty years ago. Is that right?"

"Give or take," I say.

Her bright eyes dim, tears forming. I reach out with both my hands and take hers in mine. "What's wrong?"

"I always worried that something like that happened to her."

"Who?"

"My nephew's wife."

"What happened?"

"She disappeared back then. The police suspected foul play and were going to accuse my nephew, but then he vanished. Neither were heard from again."

"I am so sorry."

"Do you think Ken can show me the pictures?"

"Why, Emelina?"

"Maybe it's not her and I can go on believing she is having a blast living on a beach in Hawaii."

"The police can do DNA testing. Maybe there are still dental records around. Or there could be something in the trunk to give them a clue as to who it was," I reply.

"She never took it off," Emelina says.

"What?"

"I gave her a necklace as a wedding present. She never took it off."

I go back to my designated cubby where I had stuffed my parka, scarf, and bag. Rummaging through my bag with nervous fingers, I find my cell phone and bring up the photo. Billy picks up on my anxiousness. He gets up from his sunny spot and begins circling my legs. I work my fingers a couple of times on the image until I am able zoom in on the necklace. The studio is empty now, save Abe. I call to Emelina, and she makes her way to Billy and me. Abe comes over and I turn the phone around to show her.

Her eyes go wide with recognition, and she collapses into Abe's arms.

CHAPTER FOUR

"You showed a hundred-year-old woman a photo of a skeleton?" Abe asks. He holds Emelina until I can grab a blanket, mat, and headrest. Once I lay everything out, he gently places her on the mat while I run for a glass of water.

Calling for an ambulance is out of the question. She simply fainted. He cradles her head while I touch the glass to her lips. Billy helps by licking her face.

"Worse, she knows who it was," I say. "Go lay down, Billy."

"Great," Abe says

"Her niece disappeared fifty years ago, and she told me that she gave her niece a necklace that she never took off."

"And that's the necklace," he says pointing to my phone on the floor.

"Yep."

"Oh boy," he says as we watch Emelina respond to the water.

"Oh boy is right," I add as I flip the phone face down.

"Oh my," Emelina says. "How long was I not here?"

"Just a few minutes," Abe says.

"Help me to sit up, Abe." Emelina orients herself to time and place.

He stays behind her until the color returns to her cheeks. The three of us sit cross-legged on the floor. Billy doesn't miss the opportunity to return and curl up inside my warm triangle and lays his head on my ankle. I pet him while we watch Emelina. The story is decades old and is not to be rushed.

"Antoinette was twenty-nine when she disappeared," she starts. "She had been married to my nephew Andrew for about five years. He was older and had a good job at Milford Specialty Steel. It went bankrupt in the Eighties. She said she had an errand to run after dinner. This was Christmas eve, 1969. We all figured she had a gift on layaway or some last-minute shopping. When we didn't hear from her, we got worried. When she didn't show up for midnight Mass, we were frantic. Back then, Milford had more police on the force, and Andrew reported her missing right after the service. The policeman was not too worried, made a note and said that if she didn't come home in forty-eight hours to go into the station and make an official report."

"That old way of thinking still prevails in some parts of the country, I'm afraid," I tell them.

"Andrew didn't wait two days. He went in Christmas morning and demanded to see the chief. He had walked around town all night calling her name to no avail."

"Did she have family?" Abe asks

"Large family. Italian Catholics. Came over on the boat. Most of them did stone masonry around town and in the city. Stone cutters in the quarries too, although the quarries are all shut down now. She was the youngest of seven. Last name was Sorrento. I am sure she is survived by some cousins." Emelina shakes her head at the memory that she now shares with us. "The chief wanted to stick to the line that Antoinette was unhappy in her marriage and with being stuck in a small town, so she lit off for the big city lights." I never saw Emelina use air quotes until this moment.

"She didn't say a word to anyone of her plans?" I ask. Billy is snoring.

"That's the thing that Andrew kept telling the chief. She didn't tell any family, friends, or co-workers of her desire to split town. She left a holiday bonus and paycheck uncashed on the dining room table. Who leaves town with just the money in their purse?"

"Where did she work?" I ask.

"She was a bookkeeper for Milford Coal & Ice. They aren't around anymore. She was a dreamy girl in high school. She was in the dramatics club and played the violin. She liked to write poetry. She even submitted a couple pieces and got them published, but her parents didn't have the money to send her to college, so her senior year at Milford High, she took bookkeeping and stenography classes." She hesitates, then stops.

"What else? You were going to say something else," I prod. I realize now as I did with Ken yesterday that I have put on my sleuthing hat. When did I go from being a concerned wife or friend to amateur detective?

I coax out more facts, using my strong confident voice. I am not asking out of politeness; I am asking to get more about the mystery of the woman in the steamer trunk. I remind myself to write this all down when I get a chance.

"Antoinette loved the movies and dragged Andrew to every new release. And the books." Emelina smiles. "I would see her every couple of weeks at the library returning a bunch and picking up as many as she could hold."

"Like what?" Abe asks.

"Mystery, adventure, romance. She was all over the place. Like I said, she was a dreamer."

"Then what happened?" I ask.

"After a while, when not a soul heard from her, the chief changed his tune and started looking at Andrew as the reason for her disappearance. My nephew was beside himself. He was the last person to see her alive, and the chief was calling him a suspect. The last thing Andrew told me was that the chief wanted to talk to him in person. Everyone said he fled town and took a new name in a different part of the country."

"Did anyone have any contact with him?"

"I met him for dinner on March 31st, 1970, and that was the last time anyone laid eyes on him, or anyone talked to him."

"How was their marriage?" Abe asks.

"You gotta remember the times we are talking about. It was the Sixties. Peace, love and happiness, psychedelics, doves and hawks. It was a time of great turmoil. Vietnam and protests were on the TV every night. Families getting torn apart by drugs, politics, boys going off to war and coming back with missing parts or in coffins."

We wait for her to finish where she was going with that thought. Emelina never dwells in the past. She is always thinking about the future. I can tell that her memory lane is rutted and runs through some dark places.

"Andrew was a hawk. He worked in a steel plant that made parts for the military. Antoinette was a sensitive soul. If she found an injured bird, she would try to nurse it back to health. So, there was that. Then there was the strain of not making babies. Her family said that she must have sinned against God. Andrew said that it wasn't his fault."

"Did either of them get tested?" I ask.

"No, it was not covered under insurance back in those days, and testing wasn't cheap."

"Did they want to have children?" Abe asks.

"I don't know what to tell you, Abe." She looks at him and avoids eye contact with me. I will follow up with her again on that topic.

"Are you sure about the necklace?" he asks.

"Positive. My nephew loved her, but he always complained

about jewelry, especially that diamond prices were fixed and overinflated. Her family was not poor, but they didn't have money for extras. Andrew and Antoinette's wedding bands were plain. He had our grandmother's engagement ring resized and gave it to her. I bought her nice earrings and that necklace as a wedding present. She adored it. She wore it every day." She pauses as her eyes well up again. "It's unique. I had it designed in the city. It was a one of a kind. I would know it anywhere."

"Do you know if they inscribed their initials and wedding date on their wedding bands?"

Emelina shakes her head and sips the rest of the water. Abe gets up and goes into the kitchen. We wait until he comes back. He brings back some steeping tea in a nice china cup on a saucer. The chai spices waft through our little seated triangle.

"Do you know their middle names?" I ask.

"Theresa and Edward."

"When were they married?"

She looks upwards and to the right. Then she looks at her hands like they are doing the arithmetic for her. "I want to say May of 1965. It was right after my mother died."

"Was Andrew suicidal before he disappeared?" The question spills out and I can't take it back.

"God, no! What are you thinking, Gwendolyn?" she blurts out and begins crying.

I've never seen Abe lose his temper, but the look he gives me has some serious curse words in them. Even Billy senses the change in mood and wakes up.

Emelina is sobbing now. I am doing a fine job of angering the people in my world.

CHAPTER FIVE

How many retired kindergarten teachers have State Police detectives on speed dial? A warmth spreads through my body. I earned the right to call this detective when I know more about his case than he does. It's not to rub it in. It's more to show him that his favorite former kindergarten teacher can run with the big dogs.

He picks up on the third ring. "Detective Shafer."

"Good morning, this is Gwendolyn Strong," I say.

There's humor in his voice. "I know, your name came up on my caller ID."

"I am calling you about the skeleton found in the steamer trunk yesterday," I say.

"Don't tell me, you already figured out who it is," he replies. The history we have earns me both his taking my call and his sarcasm.

"Actually, I am pretty sure who it is. I have someone with me now who can identify the necklace, and—"

"How do you know about the necklace?" he interrupts. "We haven't released that information to the public."

"Who discovered the body, Detective Shafer?" I ask with sugary sweetness.

"Hold on." I hear the rustle of papers. "Ken Strong. Don't tell me he's your husband."

"If he hasn't filed for divorce today, I can say that with one hundred percent certainty."

He sighs. "The body went into the trunk over fifty years ago, Mrs. Strong."

"When do you want us to come in?" I ask, ignoring his veiled objection.

"Us?"

"We come as a package deal."

"This is highly irregular, Mrs. Strong."

"Of course, it is, but have I ever let you down?"

Silence. Dead air. A deeper sigh. "I don't know. We are working on the ID now."

"Yes, I know. You are testing for DNA and have probably asked the town clerk for all marriages of persons with those initials on the month, day, and year inscribed on the inside of the ring."

"Um, sure," he stammers. I hear a plastic bag being opened. "There are no initials on the inside on the wedding band."

"Even more important that we meet." I enjoy having him give me an answer to one of my questions and one that he hadn't thought of himself. "We may be able to help you with the contents of the steamer trunk, as well." In for a penny, in for a pound.

"Sure, come over to the barracks, Mrs. Strong. Would ten o'clock be good?"

"Ten o'clock," I say aloud.

Abe, who is still holding Emelina, tenderly looks at her. Both nod.

"See you then," I say.

I disconnect the call. "Are you up for this, Emelina?"

"Yes, dear. I need to know."

"And they need to hear your story," I say.

"I'll drive," Abe tells us. Normally Emelina drives, but not today, and my Mustang will be too cramped for the four of us.

"Are you ready for a big adventure, Billy?" The doggie dance he does for me tells me he's ready.

I call Ken and it goes to voice mail. "I am sorry for how I acted yesterday. I needed to understand your, uh, situation better. You were right for being mad at me. I know that now. Give me a call when you get a chance." I stammer an "I love you," then end the message. Then I speak in a too-quiet voice to Billy. "It will be alright."

Emelina has her coat, and Abe has changed into a heavy wool sweater and corduroys over L.L. Bean boots. Billy needs a minute before we all get into Abe's silver Hyundai Sonata hybrid.

The drive out of town to the barracks is one I've have taken a few times recently. I am starting to drive more now that I have my own wheels and no longer walk to work. I had to give statements in the Stillman case and the dognapping caper there and at the District Attorney's office. Not the usual haunts for a former kindergarten teacher, I must admit.

The roads are plowed, with snow piled high on the guardrails. The highway department's salt crunches under Abe's tires. The low sun's rays hit us like a strobe light as we whisk past bare branches of tall roadside trees. We ride in that comfortable silence friends share, but also with individual apprehensions of what we will encounter. I cannot read Abe's placid demeanor. He drives with no hurry. Emelina twists her watch in deep thought. Her dour expression is so different from her usual cheeriness.

The barracks is new, thanks to grants from Homeland Security. Ample visitor parking crosses the front. Another driveway connects to the sally port in the rear of the building where they handle prisoner transfer out of the public's eye. It is an L-shaped concrete one-story structure with large planters splayed across the entrance. I am amused that the planters are empty. Plenty of funding for impediments to any wannabe bomber, but not a penny for plantings. Maybe I can talk to the Rotary or the Boy Scouts, and they can spruce things up in the spring. After 9/11, these planters popped up around governmental buildings all over the county—ugly weed-festooned objects to remind us of that terrible day.

An unidentifiable trooper behind the mirrored bullet-proof glass answers our call from the phone on the wall next to the open metal-hinged tray. Crash reports are done mostly electronically these days, and if it wasn't for my Freedom of Information requests for older records, I wouldn't need to shove money to them across this threshold.

I clearly interrupted his crossword puzzle with my pleasant singsong greeting. "Good morning. Gwendolyn Strong here for my ten o'clock with Detective Shafer."

"One moment," comes the terse reply.

At the end of the hall leading to Shafer's offices, a door opens, and Shafer and another uniformed trooper appear. Shafer says good-bye to the trooper, then motions the three of us forward.

"Detective Shafer, this is Emelina Bidwell," I say. "She can identify the owner of the necklace. Mister Schatz was nice enough to drive us today and is fully aware of the situation."

Shafer is cordial for a change. "Thank you for coming in so quickly. We appreciate you doing so, Ms. Bidwell." They must be really stumped.

He leads us through a maze of corridors to a conference room. On the conference table sits the musty steamer trunk, its contents, sans skeleton, and two plastic bags. The smell from the steamer trunk is what you would expect from a half-century of holding a decomposing body.

He slips on blue latex gloves to handle the contents. He

opens one bag and extracts the necklace. He sets it on the table under a stand with a magnification glass and fluorescent halo lighting.

Emelina takes a look through glass. "The vine leaves and grape clusters were to remind her of her Italian heritage. The gold was imported from Florence. She never took it off." Emelina blinks. "I never thought I would see it again."

"Mrs. Strong said that you had it custom made."

"Yes, it's one of a kind. I would recognize it anywhere. The floral gems are her birthstone, turquoise. See?"

Shafer bends down next to her. "When did you give it to her?"

"For her wedding to my nephew, Andrew. It was May of 1965, I believe."

"Good memory, Ms. Bidwell."

"She loved it. It was her proudest possession."

He moves to the other small plastic bag and extracts a plain wedding band.

Emelina shrugs. "They had plain bands. She was petite. This is too small for my hand," she says.

"Some of the clothing surrounding the skeleton was destroyed by the body's decomposition in an enclosed space," Shafer tells us. He is uncharacteristically polite to us. Maybe Emelina reminds him of someone. "Some air got into the trunk, but no infestation. The remnants closest to the body are being analyzed by the lab for blood type and for causes of unnatural death. These are the outer layers and what appeared to fill the trunk to its capacity."

"Newspaper and drapery," I observe.

"I don't know these drapes from anywhere," she says.

"*Milford Times Herald*?" Abe asks, looking at the newspaper.

"Milford had two newspapers for years, a morning paper and the afternoon paper, the *Milford Courier*," Emelina informs us. "Both are out of circulation now."

Shafer says, "It looks like the latest edition used as a liner was June 23, 1970."

"Andrew disappeared the last day of March 1970."

"What? Your nephew disappeared too?" Shafer asks.

"Any identification on the steamer trunk?" I interject.

Emelina defers to my question before she answers Shafer. We know it is a long answer.

"Saratoga Trunks, Saratoga, New York. Best we can tell it was made around 1870," Shafer answers us. "Is there anymore here to look at, Mrs. Strong?"

Unaccustomed to being accorded such access to the evidence, I shake my head.

"Okay then, shall we move to the interview suites? Can I get you something to drink? Tea? Coffee?"

Shafer never asks once for the name of Emelina's niece. I guess when someone is stuffed in a trunk for over fifty years, what's a few more minutes.

We walk down the hall to a brightly lit but barren room. It contains a desk and two chairs. Shafer points Emelina to take a chair that is angled to the wall with one-way glass. A camera is situated to allow a wide-angle view of both participants.

"I will take it from here, Mrs. Strong. I'd ask that you wait in the reception area," he says.

Emelina says, "I'd like them to stay with me if that is all right, Detective Shafer."

I tell her, "We'll be just on the other side of the glass, Emelina. I can understand why Detective Shafer wants to concentrate on learning as much as he can from you without any interruptions." My offer is fair to all parties. I get to listen, we are out of his hair, and Emelina knows she is not alone. Shafer's internal debate is obvious on his face. Since I am not going to be in room asking questions of her, it is still his show. Knowing that I would quiz her about what he doesn't ask her makes it obvious that I have offered a nice solution for everybody. Maybe I can stop making people angry for rest of the day.

He points to the other door and says, "That's fine. All I ask is that you wait until after I turn the recording off to ask any questions."

"Quiet as church mice, we promise."

I sit with Abe on the other side of the glass. The microphone in the interview room is turned on and broadcasts clearly his questions and her answers. I've never seen Detective Shafer at work before, and I've known Emelina my whole adult life. They are talking with their chairs angled so I can see both of their faces. I scribble notes for follow-up on the ride home. I am afraid as the interview drags on that she is flagging from the emotions and stress of the day. I will wait until after our meeting with Benjamin later this afternoon. I've never known my mentor to take an afternoon nap, but I will strongly suggest one today.

"We've covered a lot of ground, Ms. Bidwell," Shafer says eventually, looking up from his notepad. "Can I call you if I have a question or two?"

"Yes."

"This concludes the taped portion of our interview. We are going to stop recording now."

Emelina relaxes in her chair, slumping back and closing her eyes.

"I've never seen her this wiped out," Abe says.

"Me neither. She looks all of her age," I say. "Eventually walking on this earth for one hundred years will catch up with you."

"You can come in now," Shafer says to us.

We quickly come in and stand to both sides of our friend.

"Take me home, Abe. I'm tired," Emelina says. We assist her to her feet. Something we have never done for her before.

We follow Shafer through the maze back to the entrance way.

"Thank you for coming in, Ms. Bidwell," he says. "You have given me somewhere to start in figuring out what happened to Antoinette."

"You are welcome, Detective Shafer."

"And thank you, Mr. Schatz, for driving her today. It was a good idea that you did so."

"You're welcome," Abe replies.

"Good work as usual, Mrs. Strong." Shafer holds out his hand to shake mine.

"Glad to be of assistance." I pump his hand, then we let go hands but not eye contact.

I think he is trying to tell me that he's got this, and I am telling him I am prepared to do my thing. Our smiles are brief and do not linger.

Outside, the three of us are hit by a blast of arctic air that came in after the storm front had moved out yesterday. The heavy warmth of the barracks is replaced by an invigorating gust of wind on my face. Billy waits patiently in the car as the sunshine keeps the interior warm with a little cool air coming in from the cracked window. He is happy to see me, and after I let him out, we zigzag around the planters. At least they are good for something.

The interview brought up many more questions than Shafer thought to ask. I am anxious to get back to the car lest I forgot some of them. I want to rush Billy, but that never goes well. I finally bag his business and we trot back to the car.

The car is toasty. Abe motions with a finger to his lips. Emelina is fast asleep. Billy and I don't make a sound as we get in the back seat for the ride back into town.

CHAPTER SIX

We deposit Emelina at her cottage. I promise to return in time for our meeting with the Chamber president. Abe drives me home. He doesn't hold a grudge for the way I introduced her to her niece's necklace. He realizes that Em can begin properly processing her grief now after so many years of not knowing what happened.

Ken's truck is in the driveway. I am not sure he came home for a quick lunch. Billy strains his lead as we go in the front door. I unleash him and he scampers in. I return to Ken's truck for his ice scraper. I hadn't gotten one for the Mustang yet. I use a push broom to relieve a foot of snow from the convertible's soft top, then use the scraper vigorously on the windows. I can't wait to put the top down and go zooming on the interstate when the weather turns warmer.

When I'm done, I stamp snow from my boots and yell into the house, "Hi honey, I'm home."

No answer. Then the thumping of a hammer commences somewhere upstairs. Ken predictably returns to rehabbing our house when he's between jobs. With work halted on the restoration, he needs to line up more of his smaller jobs, and that requires some juggling. My socks don't make any noise on the stairs as I get to the second floor and realize he is up in the attic. He's tacking in new insulation in the rafters. "Hi honey, did you eat lunch yet?"

He nods without taking his eyes off his work.

"Did you receive my voice message?"

He nods again and finishes the row of insulation he was working on. My husband turns for the next roll. He goes to lift it up and I gently place my hand on top of it and make eye contact with him. He's wearing a mask so that none of the insulation's fiberglass gets into his throat.

"Where were you this morning?" he asks. "I've been home since ten o'clock."

"I went with Emelina to the State Police barracks, where she identified the necklace."

"What necklace?"

"The one on the… the one that fell out of the trunk yesterday." I barely avoid saying the word "skeleton" and stammer my reply.

He set down his hammer and moves to the middle of the attic where he can stand tall. "How did she know about the trunk?"

I answer him truthfully, but I have to be careful with my words, "The other yogis were talking about it after meditation this morning. They even knew that you took photos."

"How did they know that?" At least my man is talking to me. Angry, but using words instead of silence.

"Ken, it's a small town. You weren't the only one in that basement yesterday. Word gets around. If you are asking me if I told them, I can tell you that I didn't. I was a listener as much as Emelina this morning."

"And?"

"And what?" I shoot back at him.

"How did she learn about the necklace?" He has shifted gears past conversational to confrontational.

"She told me that her niece disappeared about the time the basement was partitioned off. She told me that she gave her niece a very distinctive necklace."

"And you just happened to have a picture of one."

I wish he'd take that darn mask off. "And I just happened to have a picture of one. Guilty as charged. We scheduled a visit to Detective Shafer, and she identified the actual necklace as the one she gave her niece as a wedding present in 1965."

"I don't want to know anymore, thank you very much." He picks up the roll of insulation.

"Ken?" I implore.

"No, I don't want to know anything more about it."

"You asked me where I was, and I told you. Would you rather say I walked Billy for two and a half hours?"

"What part of 'I don't want to know anything more' don't you understand?"

"Do you want to keep me company while I eat?" I ask.

"I already ate." He turns his back to me and starts tacking the next roll between the rafters.

I'd hate to be one of those tacks. I retreat downstairs with Billy right behind me. He goes where the food is.

I replay the conversation over in my head as I fill his food dish. I slather too much mustard on my ham and cheese on rye and it burns my tongue. I dump too many chips on my plate and Billy gets a few that spilled to the floor—a bonus for him. I eat alone to the tap, tap, tap from above. There is a lot to chew on, literally and figuratively.

"Why is Ken upset with me, Billy?" The dog only looks at me, expecting some of my sandwich won't quite make it to my mouth. "Some companion you are," I lament.

Okay, yesterday Erin and I were amateur detectives, and today I helped the State Police identify the skeleton that had played jack in the box with my beloved husband. Mid-bite, I realize once more that for me this event is a mystery to be solved, a case to work on, or at least a question to be answered. For Kenneth Strong, a remodeler and Milford's best handyman, it was something terribly ghoulish and totally out of whack with his everyday life. He wishes he never manhandled that steamer. He wants to stuff the evil genie back in the lamp, but I keep rubbing it.

Is it possible for me to leave this matter to the capable hands of Detective Shafer? I can ask Emelina on the case progress from time to time. We can learn about things in the way a small town operates.

Jimmy in the lumber yard can ask Ken, "Isn't that something about the skeleton you found, Mr. Strong?" Maybe I will be standing in line at the convenience store getting a Mega Millions lottery ticket and reading the ticker on the all-news station playing above the clerk's head. On the flat screen, I will see the breaking news on a fifty-year-old murder. When the memories fade—and hopefully the nightmares don't emerge—he and I can talk about it.

Two paths emerge before me. One requires only Emelina's permission to continue. I can inform my husband that I am working at her request, and I will promise to spare him all the gory details. The other is that I leave it to the professionals. After all, what do I know about solving cold cases? "What do I know about solving cold cases, Billy?" I repeat out loud to my little amigo.

He cocks his head quizzically. He is so cute.

"Actually," I continue, "I know something about cold cases, and I know a couple of people who know a heck of a lot more."

I text Erin to call me when quiet time starts in her household. I make my decision. Erin or I will talk with FBI agent Marsha O'Shea, whom we worked with on the New Haven cold case. I'm sure she will have some pointers for us. Ken made no demands on me other than he doesn't want to know anything more about it.

I change into nicer clothes. I choose a pleated skirt and cashmere sweater over matching tights. It always worked for parent-teacher conferences.

I tell Billy to go see Ken while I go outside and start the car. The V-8 comes to life with a rumble. I dash back inside and run up all the stairs. I burst into the attic and interrupt Ken again. I run up to him, pull the mask off one ear, and plant a kiss on his lips. "I promise I won't say another word to you about what happened yesterday or this morning. Emelina and I are going to the Chamber of Commerce. We are trying to get them to have us cater the desserts for the President's Day party."

"Okay," he manages.

"I'll try to get a cookie or two for you. Would you like that?"

"You know my weak spot. That's not fair." He tries not to smile.

"As if you don't know mine." I wink at him, then squeeze him hard. "I will be home in time to start dinner." It's a start. I don't know if he is thawing or if I am wishful.

A short time later, I knock on Emelina's door. she looks better. A nap and a bite to eat have perked her up. She too changed clothes, and we both look presentable. More importantly, I carefully place several tins of her desserts in the backseat. I honestly don't think we have to sell the product, only the price, and I will leave that to her. I only have one question for her before I turn off the car in the Chamber's near-empty parking lot downtown.

"Would you like me to find out what happened to Antoinette?"

"I like Detective Shafer," she says.

"I like him better now after I watched him interview you. I think he will do his best." I try not to act crestfallen.

"I was saying I like Detective Shafer, but I know you won't let me down," she says. Elation gives way to the worry. What if I do let her down? She's my mentor and new business partner. Be careful what you ask for, Gwendolyn Strong.

CHAPTER SEVEN

Benjamin Bloodstone is a small wiry man in his late seventies. He has been the president of the Chamber of Commerce for as long as I can remember. He sits on almost every philanthropic board in Milford, and his name is synonymous with optimism and good cheer. "Hello, Emelina, how are you?"

She looks at me and then back to him, saying, "I learned some bad news today, I am afraid."

He leads her to two upholstered chairs in the reception area. I take some of the tins from her and place all our tins on the reception counter. Business will have to wait.

"What's the matter, Emelina?" he asks. "I have never seen you this upset."

The tiredness returns to her voice. "By now you have heard about the discovery at the old Devlin mansion."

It still goes by the name of the Civil War hero who became one of the state's longest running U.S. Senators. Patrick Devlin was a contemporary of Taylor Bloodstone, Benjamin's great-great grandfather.

"Terrible business. Yes, I heard."

"Gwendolyn's husband made the discovery."

"It must have been quite a shock," he says.

"It was. Something he would rather forget," I say truthfully.

Emelina says, "A relative of mine went missing about the same time as work was done in the mansion's basement." She looks from Benjamin to me and then inwardly. "I found out today that the woman was Antoinette, my niece." Then she bursts into tears.

Benjamin scoops her into his arms and gives her a long hug. His face is turned away from me, and I watch as abject grief overcomes my mentor. She is sobbing a gut-heaving sob and it's all Benjamin can do to hold her erect. *Why are there never tissues handy when you need them?* I run to the unisex bathroom, grateful it is not occupied, and tear off an arm's length of toilet paper and dash back to them.

"It was the necklace that she never took off," Emelina is telling Benjamin. "I gave it to her as a wedding present." I was not privy to the first part of the conversation. They are seated again, and I hand her the wad of toilet paper. Benjamin is attempting to comfort her. He is usually smiling and bubbly, a genuinely happy selfless servant to the community. He serves Emelina by sharing in her grief. I would call them acquaintances and not friends, and I am envious at how easily he comforts her. Ken needed a wife, not an amateur sleuth yesterday. Did I forfeit my friendship with Emelina in the rush to find out more about Antoinette? Abe is a new friend, and Ben is an old one. When did I put friendship behind finding the truth?

"Of course, you have every right to be upset, you thought she had run off on your nephew," Benjamin says, looking over her shoulder towards me. "You are just finding this out now." He holds her one hand tightly as she wipes her eyes.

If by some form of transference, he shares her grief and tries to restrain his own sobs. I hand him the remaining paper as both close their eyes into the damp toilet paper. Instinctively, I kneel between them. I place a gentle hand on top of their clasped hands. Sometimes, being a kindergarten teacher is just about holding hands and maintaining eye contact.

"I'm sorry Benjamin, I am being an old lady," Em sniffles.

"Nonsense. Better to let it all out when you are surrounded by friends." He smiles through red-rimmed teary eyes and nods to me.

On cue, I say, "That's right, we are here for you Emelina."

She shakes her head. "I haven't even notified her next of kin."

"Detective Shafer will take care of that," I say robotically. "It's his job."

Benjamin looks at me quizzically. "Why are the police involved?"

"It is a suspicious death. There is no statute of limitations for a homi—uh, something like this." I steer away from the more inflammatory word.

"I see." A pause. "What can I do for you, Emelina? How can I help?"

"I don't know." She is slowly gathering herself. "I don't know."

It hits us that this was not a social visit. Benjamin is first to speak. "It was just a formality for you to come in. Truth be told, everyone here kept asking me all morning when you were going to bring in your treats. It was just an excuse to sample some of your goodies. You have the contract, dear, and I will personally donate whatever you think is fair."

"I will call on you to get the details tomorrow," I say. "We will need to know how many we are baking for."

"We?" he asks

"Yes, I've asked Gwen to be in business with me," she says.

We all smile. I know why my eyes are not red-rimmed and leaking tears. Will dealing with another dead body deaden my feelings even more?

"Splendid. See me tomorrow, Mrs. Strong. I will be here in the afternoon."

"I'll come by for the tins after lunch. I am sure they will be empty by then."

His red eyes twinkle as he says, "You can bet your bottom dollar on that."

I rise from my kneeling position while Ben and Emelina find their feet and stand on wobbly legs. She has never looked this old to me. Maybe I never wanted to admit it, but my mentor will not be with me forever. Maybe this is why she asked me to help her with baking her secret recipes. Maybe helping her with what happened to Antoinette will be my last thank you for all she has done for me.

We make our way back to my car. I should have started it. The temperature has dropped even more as the sun dips behind the mountain overlooking Milford. The polar express howling down from the north along the river is going to send real temperatures below zero.

Normally, I wouldn't walk Emelina to her cottage, but today is not a normal day. I want to make sure she is okay, that the heat is working, that there is a dinner planned along with anything else that needs tending to. I helped her once when she caught the flu bug, but in all the time I've known her, she has made it clear to anybody who would listen that she is an independent lady who can take care of herself. I feel guilty about the two—I'm lying, three chocolate chip cookies I pinched for Ken. I need some help today myself.

"Well, that went well," she says. "I can name my own price and decide what to make."

"All we need is the numbers," I say cheerfully.

She sits in her favorite chair by the window. There is not a TV to be found in her house. I find the tea and add water to the kettle. There is a plate of sugar cookies on kitchen counter, and I bring them out to the side table next to her chair.

"How are you fixed for dinner tonight?" I ask.

"I was going to pick something up from Bill at the Country Market after yoga…" Her voice trails off.

"How about I treat my favorite kindergarten teacher to dinner out? I haven't treated you in a long time."

"I don't know, Gwen."

"Besides, Ken will be less grumpy if I bring him some take out." I sort of kind of didn't want to use the word *grumpy*, but it was what I was thinking.

"Grumpy?"

"Since yesterday, he has been dealing with his own emotions of what happened, and…" Here I am bringing up my petty marital squabble to a woman whose relative by marriage was stuffed in a box and forgotten like a New Year's resolution.

"And I haven't been supportive," I finish up.

"You look at things differently now, Gwen."

I didn't take it as an indictment, just a statement of fact. "Erin and I looked at the photos for clues. He just wanted us to feel sympathy for what he went through. Even today, Em, I was all business until you talked to Benjamin about it." I shake my head at the change. "Where did my mindful listening go?"

"Many people went to Jake's and Brian's funerals to offer their sympathies." She's talking about the Stillman murders I had helped solve. "How many of them figured out both boys were murdered and who committed the crimes?" she asks me.

"How come you know how to say what I need to hear every time?"

"Abe said you had a gift. Erin and I see it too. It will take Ken some time to get used to the changes. Give him time."

Abe would be proud of the deep cleansing breath I take. It releases the clenched grip on my gut. Emelina is right, of course.

My oldest friend sees the gift, where I just see a soft-boiled detective ignoring the feelings of the people closest to me.

The freezing wind howls outside, but for now, the warmth of friendship, tea, and hissing radiators settles on us as we sit in thoughtful silence.

CHAPTER EIGHT

I try not to analyze the urgency of our lovemaking as Ken and I catch our breath. I should bring him shrimp scampi and Emelina's chocolate chip cookies more often. Sometimes words fail when action speaks volumes. Love and desire were never our problem. The way we act out our stubbornness is usually the culprit.

"It is a good thing what you are doing for Emelina," he says as he stares at the ceiling. "But I still don't want to know about it. The sooner I can forget what was in that trunk, the happier I will be."

"What if it was me at the school while going through trunks in the basement?" I say, two days later than I should have.

"Exactly, and how would you feel?" he asks.

"Terrified, especially if a pupil were helping me."

I roll onto my side facing him and place my hand on his rapidly beating heart. I am glad I still do that to him. "What bothers me is that I've gotten cold and analytical about death."

"Bothers me too," he says. My guy places his rough hand gently on mine.

"I was supposed to work for eight more years and figure out what I wanted to do in retirement."

"Do you regret giving up your position? You had seniority to keep your job," he says.

"What? And have them lay off a pregnant twenty-something who is the best kindergarten teacher this school district could ever hope to attract?"

"No doubt you left the kids in good hands, Gwen. I am just saying."

"You are saying it's just as much an adjustment for you as it was for me," I realize.

"Things happened so fast since after the board meeting when they decided to close the school."

"Well, I did find Abe's meditation and yoga studio, and let's not forget about Billy." The dog is snoring in his crate at the foot of our bed. No sleeping in our bed for the little guy. Both Ken and I agree on that.

"All good things to fill your time," he says.

"But that is what they are. Time fillers."

"Emelina is going to show you how to bake her secret recipes," he says, squeezing my hand.

"I know where I will be bringing all the mistakes or ugly ones," I squeeze back.

"You better."

"What do you think about my new vocation?"

He takes a deep breath, then sighs. "If it was Erin, I could understand it better. Sherlock Holmes doesn't have anything on our favorite daughter."

I laugh at a familial joke. Erin is our only daughter.

"I married a kindergarten teacher," he continues, "and you married a handyman."

"I always said you were handy, Ken."

"What if I figured out that I could be a private investigator?" he asks.

"You'd have to explore it, of course. I wouldn't stand in your way if that is what you wanted to do." I realize that I never had a heart to heart with him about my switch in vocations.

"We never really talked about it, but now would be a good time, don't you think? You helped Erin out with that thing in New Haven. Then your curiosity got the best of you with Brian and Jake, and before you knew it, you got the show dog back for Mrs. Pearce. Now we are wrestling with this thing."

"This thing involves you too, honey."

"I know. I'd like to forget it, but I never will."

"So, my sticking my nose into it doesn't let you forget it."

"That's about the size of it," he says.

"But there is more to it, isn't there, babe?" I ask.

"Part of me realizes where Erin got her smarts from for this sort of thing, but the other part of me worries about you."

"Because I am sticking my nose where it doesn't belong."

"Not so much that as you haven't been trained in self-defense or have the power of the badge to protect you."

"And you can't always be there to protect me."

He turns to face me in the flickering candlelight. "It's more than that. Until..." He chokes back a cough. "Until recently, I thought that you would outlive me and become Milford's oldest person. This thing that you do, you are really good at it, but I didn't sign up for it. I didn't have any say in it, and face it, Gwen, this stuff puts you in harm's way. I don't know what I would do without you." He pulls me on top of him and I let him. He needs to hide his face. We hold each other in pensive stillness.

Finally, I rise to my elbows. "If you don't want me to pursue this case and just bake with Emelina, I will."

He shakes his head. "That's the point. It's not my decision. I can't have you harbor resentment at me for telling you to stop doing this stuff. I see how you are. You light up like the sky at the town's Fourth of July fireworks display when you discuss new clues with Erin. You are like a dog with a bone when you solve these puzzles."

I know there is more coming. He says, "Remember, I was there that day when you told Detective Shafer that we stumbled onto a murder scene and to treat it as such. I watched what you did until the police arrived. I can't be so selfish to tell the woman I love what she can and cannot do. It has to be your decision."

"I don't want to leave you as Milford's most eligible widower, either. I want to be with you for a long time." I kiss him long and hard. There was a time when we were younger, and the kids were zonked, that there would be more than a candle aflame at this hour.

"Let me sleep on it," I add. I kiss him gently and roll off. On the way back from the bathroom, I blow out the candle.

I am worried when Emelina doesn't show up for meditation. I can't concentrate on my breath. Billy senses my uneasiness. We get up and stretch, then I go to the kitchen and call her. After several rings on her landline, an old-fashioned analog answering machine picks up. I leave a message telling her we miss her at the studio and to call Abe or me. I am not sure what to do, but we put on our layers anyhow. Billy doesn't like his sweater and gives me the most baleful stare, but temps are around zero with a wind chill in minus double digits.

We scurry to Emelina's cottage. Her car is not there. The front door is locked. There is no sign of forced entry with the windows. I make sure each one is locked. The back door is locked, and the basement windows are all secure. "Billy, I am not being paranoid, honest," I say. I have nothing to write on, so we go back down the driveway out to the street and cross the street to the Fletcher house, where I knock.

"Hi, Mr. Fletcher," I say as I stamp my feet on his porch. Billy is peeking out of my puffy parka. "Did you see when Emelina left?"

"No, you just woke me up with all that racket, Mrs. Strong."

"Sorry. Can I borrow a piece of paper and a pen?"

"Why?"

"I want to leave her a message that I stopped by."

"Doesn't she have a phone?"

"I left her a message, but I am not sure she always checks the phone with all those telemarketers calling old people."

"Old-ER people, Mrs. Strong. Old-ER."

"Yes, sir. Older people," I correct myself.

"Wait here," he says.

"Sure." I say. I'll just pretend it's a fine summer's day, Mr. Fletcher. I literally bite my tongue as the cold seeps in.

He returns with a scrap of paper and a pencil with a dull point.

I smile, thank him, and traipse back to her door. Standing there, my fingers, sans mittens, start to tingle. I try wedging the folded piece of paper into the doorjamb near the lock when I hear her old Mercury arrive.

She pulls up and sees me on her porch. Emelina lowers her window. I put the note in my pocket. I think she had to roll it down. "Doc Cleary wants to talk to you, Gwen."

Doctor Thomas Cleary is the county coroner. I start to her car, then remember my midnight conversation with Ken. I stop. Emelina looks at me with a quizzical frown.

"Can we drop Billy off at the house?" I ask. "I have to run in and tell Ken something. It will only take a second."

CHAPTER NINE

"The hyoid bone was fractured. Absent any other obvious cause of death, my ruling will be homicide, death by strangulation." Doc Cleary doesn't need to know that Erin told me about where the hyoid bone sits in the neck and how it can be a clue when looking at strangulations. I swear after that podcast about serial killers was finished, I could not wear anything snug against my throat. Just getting tangled in my bedsheets causes me to panic.

I am not sure that Emelina should be here, but she fetched me when Cleary told her he was ready to make the determination. Why she was there so early in the morning is still unclear to me, but Shafer told us the previous day that Doc Cleary was undertaking the post-mortem.

"I know you don't want me to ask this, Emelina," I say, "but what about a death by suicide hanging?"

Doc Cleary arches an eyebrow at me but gives me a straightforward answer, nonetheless. "I can't completely rule it out, but given how the body was found in a trunk hidden behind a wall, I can't imagine someone wanting to cover up a suicide, can you Mrs. Strong?"

"No, we can't." Emelina answers for us too quickly, and I don't object.

"Even if I didn't know how the body was found," he continues, "with a young, otherwise healthy female, we don't see many hyoid bone fractures with suicide hangings."

"Have you told Detective Shafer yet?" I ask.

"I have some more observations to note, but I will phone him with my preliminary findings shortly."

I am not sure how I want to phrase my next question to him, and he senses it. "Mrs. Strong, is there something the matter?"

"No, the opposite. Why—" I just decide to ask him point blank. "Why did you have her fetch me?"

He reaches for his blue Yale Medical School coffee cup and ponders my question. "I knew Antoinette's family growing up. Shafer hadn't bothered to catch me up with her identity. I learned that this morning," he says, pointing to Emelina.

"She'll need a proper burial. That is why I came over to see Doc Cleary—to find out when he will release her," she says to me. "I told Doc you were going to find out what happened."

The doctor looks from her to me and says, "At first, my nose was out of joint when you proved me wrong on Jake's murder. No doubt Brian's death would have been ruled accidental if you hadn't been involved." He brings up the case that brought me local notoriety. Then he changes the topic. "I know that you and Emelina are very close. It's important that we find out exactly what happened, Mrs. Strong, don't you think?" He stares at me above the rim of the coffee cup.

I would be lying if I said I don't get a jolt of electricity through my body when a professional acknowledges my newfound talents. I suppress a smile and just nod. "Call me Gwen."

Erin and my adorable grandchildren meet Emelina and me at the County Public Library. It's a newer building with a lovely children's section. My father, Stan Wallin, has offered to chaperone them while we work the microfilm machines. We get the kids settled and meet the research librarian, Mary Beth Botto, who says, "I have the microfilm for both papers for 1969 and 1970. I loaded up Jan-Jun 1969 on both machines." She points to the money changer next to the photocopier. "You can break your bills into quarters there and pop them in here. It is twenty-five cents a page."

Erin and I take our seats, and Em sits between us. Mary Beth, who I taught in kindergarten and watched grow up, is one the bright ones who went on to college and returned home. "Ms. Bidwell," she says, "wait until the frame of the newspaper on the screen stops before looking, otherwise it will make you dizzy." Turning to us, she adds, "Once you have framed what you want copied on the screen, press the green button, but make sure you have enough quarters in the queue."

Erin asks, "And the Milford High School yearbooks?"

"I have them at my desk when you need them. 1958 through 1965," Mary Beth replies.

"And the Coles directories?" Erin asks.

"Those books are in year order and are kept in the cage. I will let you in, but anything in that room stays, in the room, capisce?"

"Capisce," Emelina says and then asks, "What are the Coles directories?"

"They are like a telephone book on steroids. Not only do they list telephone numbers and addresses in alphabetical order by person's last name, but they also list residents at every address in Milford by street name alphabetically," Erin tells her.

"Sometimes you can find out if someone died, got married, or was removed from the directory," Mary Beth adds. "I will leave you to it." She kneels next to Emelina and says, "I am sorry for your loss. If there is anything more I can do, just let me know." She scurries back to her desk to answer a ringing phone.

Erin tells us, "Today, we are just trying to get a feel for what it was like living here when Antoinette disappeared. If we spot young people who are getting recognized for achievements, who may still be alive, make a copy. If we see something that piques our curiosity, make a copy. If we see anything about the Devlin house, make a copy."

We get busy on the machines. We stop when we see something of note and Emelina gives us the color commentary. I did not grow up here and am fascinated by what the town looked like before I arrived.

I was born in the mid-Sixties in England on a Royal Air Force base to a black Jamaican nurse and the wonderful white man in the children's room across the hall. My mother returned to her home country when I was six, and it was not until some years later that my father returned to the States, where he met my stepmom, Jean, and settled in this neck of the woods as an Air Force recruiter.

It was not until 1985 that I came to Milford as a college senior doing student teaching and met my mentor, Emelina. She taught me everything I learned about teaching kindergarten, and when I was ready, she retired, but she was never far from me, and I could always lean on her for support.

Seeing a snapshot of Milford through the newspapers of that tumultuous time in America was truly educational. Grainy black and white photos of the ground war in Vietnam were on the front pages next to articles about the war's progress. President Nixon talked about foreign trade policy and domestic issues. The morning paper Erin's scanning is more liberal, while the afternoon paper whirling on my reader is more conservative as we compare news stories on the same subjects. Small town Milford was just starting to loosen up. People with long hair were not called hippies anymore; some were professionals, like a schoolteacher standing next to projects from the science fair. Fishing season brought with it pictures of happy anglers holding up unlucky trout from the area's streams. Baseball, especially high school and American Legion dominated the sports pages. What blew me away were the prices. A gallon of gas was thirty-one cents. A whopper at Burger King was forty-nine cents and fries were a quarter. My Mustang sold new back then for $3,900.

"I could feed my family on under fifty a week," Erin murmurs when I tell her the price of a pound of ground round.

Both of us print off the police blotter and any articles about serious crimes. Policeman's names are listed. No female officers back then. Anytime a cop was given an award for valor or heroism, we punched the green button. Mary Beth comes over and refills the copier's paper tray.

The business section of my paper handled stock prices, charts on the commodities, and news items about local businesses. A man's face and overbearing stature become repetitive to me.

"Burgess Bloodstone shows up a lot in the business section. Is he related to Benjamin?"

"It's his father. He died when you were just starting out here," Emelina says.

I press the copy button when Mary Beth gives me the thumbs up.

"He was an unhappy man. He was older than me. Blamed foreign competition and a downturn in the economy for his problems. The Bloodstone family fortune dwindled with him at the reins. But you wouldn't know it by how he held court at the county club. He had a brand-new black Cadillac every year."

"Not a big fan, huh?" Erin asks without taking her eyes off the scanning. She is already on Jul-Dec 1969, while I am still looking at Memorial Day sales.

"He was pro-business and felt the town should spend money on attracting new businesses to the area. He was tough on social spending. He thought that teacher's salaries were an expense to be controlled, just like his factory workers. No, Erin, I was not a fan to say the least."

"Well, it looked like Benjamin turned out okay," I say.

"Benjamin was an only child and they had high expectations of him to marry and keep producing Bloodstones. I think Benjamin stayed single and didn't have offspring just to spite the old man. His father was demanding of all around him, and I don't doubt that he treated everybody like a servant, including Ben."

Emelina's energy returns from the low of these past couple of days as the newspaper articles spark her already excellent memory. The microfilm whirls. April comes over and sits on Emelina's lap as we feed quarters into the photocopier.

"I took the liberty of copying the senior class still portraits for the years in question. I did the Catholic school too," Mary Beth tells us. She hands us a sheaf of printed copies and points to the clock. "No charge."

Emelina is grateful and asks, "Do you have any food allergies?"

"Molasses. Why?"

I know that rules out a tin of gingerbread cookies.

"I'd like to bake you a proper thank you," Emelina replies.

"I couldn't accept," Mary Beth says.

"Just put them on the counter and tell people that Emelina Bidwell made a donation to the library," she says, smiling.

"I can do that," the young librarian replies, smiling back. Another place for a business card or two for our yet to be named business.

Before I know it, Mary Beth tells us it's closing time. Where did the time go? My father, Caleb, and Jesse emerge from their time spent with time-traveling dinosaurs and pirate adventurers.

Working a cold case murder investigation with Erin and Emelina is fun. I'm jazzed. I never felt this energetic after a long day at school. We head for the front door and a dark cold night.

CHAPTER TEN

Ken is on his own for dinner. He doesn't want to hear about what I did today. Erin and I must make sense of what we copied. He wasn't happy when I told him that I would be helping Emelina solve the fifty-year-old murder of Antoinette Sorrento Bidwell, but he didn't stand in my way either. Some spouses might object or worse. We talk with words and not our hands. Neither of us takes the other for granted, and we still genuinely love each other fiercely and show it like the other night. But still, poking around in matters "best handled by the police," as he is sometimes told by trades people he deals with, makes for awkward conversations, especially after I handle things better than the people who wear a badge. I did promise him that I would sign up for a self-defense class and carry a personal alarm/mace combo sooner rather than later.

I drive to Erin's house and eat sloppy joes and Tater Tots with her bunch. It's a weeknight, and she had no time to prepare a nicer meal. Her husband, Darren, gets to do bath time, but the three of us have one child each to read bedtime stories to before she and I get back to the digging.

"The technology has gotten better for optical character

recognition, or OCR as it's called. The archive search site Newspaper Archives is very robust and getting better all the time," she tells me. "Let's plug in a name or two and see what pops up."

I shuffle through my photocopies and proffer, "Herman Kenrick. He was the Chief of Police back then. I have dozens of photos of him handing out awards or swearing in new officers."

Erin types in his name and filters for twenty years in both directions from 1970. "487 hits. Looks like the last ones are his obituary in Lakeland, Florida in 1979." She quickly builds an Evernote folder and sends the PDFs to document storage software.

"One more," she says.

"Burgess Bloodstone," I say.

"Wow! This guy was busy. 1,079 entries from 1937 to 1987, when he died," she says. Thinking for a moment with her hands poised above the keyboard, she asks, "What was the program that Kate and Marsha used in New Haven? Do you remember? I helped them with finding law school alumni from the late 1990s. It has everything we need to store names and index them. Gives us a timeline too."

I shake my head. "I will find out." I retrieve my phone.

"Gwen, how is my favorite amateur sleuth?" my favorite FBI agent, Marsha O'Shea, asks after we exchange hellos on the phone.

"I'll tell Erin you are asking for her," I say. Marsha always has a way of making me blush.

"You've had some fun since the last time we worked together," she tells me. "Erin keeps me up to date."

I give a raised eyebrow to my daughter. "Well, she does contract for the FBI, so I am sure she might have reason or two to chat with you, Special Agent O'Shea."

"What's up, Gwen? How can I help?"

"The software you used on the New Haven case, what was it called?"

"*CaseSoft.*"

"How much is it?" I ask.

She laughs. "I used the company credit card. I got it with all the bells and whistles. I didn't bother to price it."

I tell Erin the software name, then she types and whistles. "How serious are you about your hobby, Mom?" Erin shows me the website.

I look at the price. "Ouch. I can't tell your father I am putting that on our credit card."

"It's a business expense," Marsha says.

"Except I don't have a business, remember. I need a PI license."

We sit at the crossroads. I can't use index cards for a half-century-old murder. What worked on the Stillman case doesn't apply here, and that is when it hits me.

"I might be able to pull in a favor," I tell Marsha. "Do you remember that criminal defense attorney you talked to on my behalf?"

"Your first case?"

"Yes, that's the one."

Erin and I talk with her for a few more minutes about the case, and she gives us a few more tips before she asks about Ken and I ask about her Joe, her partner. We ring off.

I type an email to the defense attorney who assisted me on the Stillman case. At the time, we had argued good-naturedly of who was assisting whom, but I refused to be part of her defense of the Stillman brother charged with two homicides.

It's after nine p.m. and I don't expect a reply. In the time I tell Erin what I am doing, my phone pings. The reply email reads,

So good to hear from you Gwendolyn. Yes, we use CaseSoft all the time, usually for Federal drug cases when we get tons of

phone and wire intercept transcripts. Here is the link. I have restricted access to you only for your own cases. Good luck. Let me know how it turns out. Remember Spencer's invitation to put you on his license.

I forward the email to Erin. "It's only for our own stuff, Mom," she says. "I can't eyeball any of her cases whatsoever. The Bureau would frown on that."

"Yes, that is what she said too."

"We will have to do our own data input. Are you sure you want to go down this route?" she asks.

I think about it. This is way different than Billy and I walking around town and talking to people. Erin and I have to learn Antoinette's connection around town in the years before her death. Marsha is telling me that we have to find the connections and then the interconnections between the people who knew her. A stranger in town would not know to hide the body in the Devlin mansion. That person would have to have intimate knowledge of the renovations to know that the room was being partitioned off.

I was never one for seat work. I learned to do student evaluations as efficiently as possible. Sitting for hours on end doing data input is not my idea of how to spend a winter's day. I know the difference between the easy way and the right way.

"How else will we see the forest from the trees, Baby?" I tell Erin. I pick up a photocopy from my stack and pull one from her stack, then for good measure I take one from the high school yearbooks. I lay the three pieces of paper down like pieces to a puzzle. "How will I remember where I learned something, and where do I search for the connection that I saw during the review to know these three pieces of paper are connected?"

She nods. "Better still, with the OCR, some of the connections will be made for you and you don't have to rely on your memory. We only have to do the input of this paper once, along with all the articles I find in Newspaper Archives."

"You are offering to help me?" I ask.

"It's darn cold outside, Mom, what else is there to do? Let's get all this stuff entered and then we figure out who knew Antoinette and if they are still alive. I can't imagine there are that many."

"How much do we involve Emelina?" I ask.

My daughter doesn't hesitate. "Every step of the way. Before we talk to anybody, we should consult with the Oracle."

"The Oracle?"

"Greek mythology and *The Matrix* movies. For our purposes, it's Emelina. How many small towns have a centenarian who lived there all their life and taught kindergarten to half the population? She knows so much more than we would ever learn from all these newspaper articles, and more importantly, she can make the connections."

"What do you think are our chances, Erin?" I ask.

"It's hard to say. A cold case that was never investigated in the first place is not going to be easy. We are going to find out how difficult it will be to recreate her life from fifty years ago."

"We've only scratched the surface and look what we have so far. This is going to be a ton of work," I say. I look at the CaseSoft program opened on her one screen with over a thousand articles written about just one person, albeit a prominent person in town whose photo is staring at me from her laptop. The three stacks of photocopied articles and yearbook pictures from the library are several inches tall. None of the folks we will be talking with went to kindergarten during my tenure. They will be from my mentor's era. "I promised Emelina I would look into it for her."

"When do we get started on this?" she asks.

"I'll bring Emelina here after yoga tomorrow." I already kissed and hugged my adorable grandchildren. I thank Darren for giving his wife and me time to sort this out. A new quest is starting. Where it will end up, I haven't a clue, but I do know that

Emelina, Erin, and I are a force to be reckoned with, and Milford better be prepared.

I step outside into the dead still night air. The stars shine brightly overhead. The moon dances in and out of scattered clouds. The Mustang roars to life, and I warm up in about ten minutes as I make my way home, hopefully to a warmer bed and an even warmer embrace.

CHAPTER ELEVEN

Billy and I walk to meditation class and then he has fun doing "up dog" to everyone's "down dog" during yoga. Who knew my little rescue would become the darling wherever I go? In some parts of town, I am simply Billy's owner. He has his own entourage now of people that come out of their houses to give him treats. He hops into his snuggly bed while Emelina and I assist Abe with putting things away.

"We need your help, Emelina, if we want to make heads or tails of what we are looking at. I don't want to make it complicated, but we decided to scan all the paperwork we collected at the library yesterday into a computer application that will help us sort it and keep track of everything. It also has a timeline feature that will help us keep the facts in perspective."

"When do we start?" Her eyes brighten at the thought of doing something productive about her murdered niece.

"Erin said we could go down to her house as soon as we can. Do you have any other plans?"

"I was hoping we could bake something in this lovely kitchen so we see how we work together."

"How can I argue with that?" Baking with Emelina has benefits. "What do you have in mind?"

"A batch of chocolate chip cookies. I have all the ingredients in the refrigerator."

"Can Ken have a couple?" I ask.

"Of course, dear. I want to thank him for allowing you to help me with Antoinette."

I look at her with mock anger. "I don't need his permission to help you."

"Just the same, I think a dozen will help smooth things out, don't you think?" She winks at me.

"I'll text him to swing by when they are fresh out of the oven and you can tell him yourself," I say.

"Deal."

"Can I help?" Abe offers. A retired commodities trader, Mister Schatz came to Milford to rebuild his health and life with yoga and meditation after years of chasing pork bellies and wheat futures in the city.

Emelina looks at me and says, "No, Abe, this is just for Gwendolyn and me"

"I meant with Antoinette. I know the story from what you told Detective Shafer, and I can help with all the paperwork. I have a good eye for detail."

"I need a good eye for detail," I say before she can object. I dread the idea of having to read blurry newsprint for hours on end. With Emelina and Erin there to back me up, I feel Abe would be a welcome addition.

"Great. I will change and drive us all when the cookies are done."

There is no recipe book, as Emelina does it all by memory. I do exactly as I am instructed. She tells me some of her secrets, and they have to do with butter, lots of real butter. Before long, the state-of-the-art kitchen and studio is filled with the unmistakable aroma of baking cookies. Billy hopes for some cookie dough or crumbles, but Emelina sets the rules early for my mooching pooch. Not sure he will be allowed anywhere near this kitchen when we get the food license.

Ken pulls in out front with a screeching stop. I remember that hunger when we were first dating and planned to sneak off to our favorite parking spot.

"Hello, Ken," she says.

"Hi Emelina," he replies. He stares at the first batch cooling on tray the way he did at me when I first wore a plunging neckline on a date.

"I'd like you to have these. I know you will never forget what you saw at the Devlin mansion, but I want you to know that I will never forget how your lovely wife is helping me through this tragedy."

I spatula twelve into a tin and say, "This one didn't turn out okay. Would you like it now?" I make sure not to blink as it goes from my hand to his hand to his mouth. I won't say aloud what the look on his face reminds me of.

After he swallows, he says, "I'm back in the mansion today. The police have allowed me to pull apart the coal furnace and remove it. Finally."

This is news to me. We have kept certain topics off limits.

Abe comes down from his studio apartment and asks, "Ready?"

Ken looks at us.

"We're going to Erin's house for the day. Not sure what time we will be home." I peck him on the cheek. We all make our way to the front door and Abe turns the lights off and sets the alarm.

Billy doesn't know whether to go with Ken or me, but since I have the leash, he toddles along with us.

"Thank you for thinking of me, Ms. Bidwell," Ken says and shakes the tin.

"You're welcome, Ken."

I fill in Abe and Emelina in on our work for the day as we head off to Erin's house. She is home-schooling my adorable grandchildren this morning, and their other grandmother, Samantha LeGrande, is coming over for the afternoon for a play date. "Abe, you will read and scan all the paper into the software program. Erin and I will create the tags for the names it recognizes as well as dates and short notes. Then with all the names, we will use the Newspaper Archives program to unearth more articles from before and after the timeframe Antoinette went missing. As we three do the play-by-play, Emelina will add the color commentary."

Abe says, "Sounds like a plan."

"I like it," Emelina adds.

"Our goal will be to find connections to Antoinette with any persons of interest. Then the hard work will start where we run their names against the Social Security Death Index, get obituaries if they are dead, or locate them if they are still alive. We need to create a working snapshot of her world back then." I take a deep breath. "The people who are in town, we will talk to face-to-face. Out of towners, we will call by phone after dinner. This process can take a couple days or a week. It depends on what we find and how many people from back in the day are still alive."

Emelina looks out the side window and says frankly, "It should be pretty easy for me to tell you who's left. I can count my younger contemporaries on one hand. I've been to every funeral in town since I retired, so run the names by me first. You and I have taught most of the living residents of Milford, Gwen. You know the kids you taught and their parents. I probably taught the parents and knew *their* parents. Between us, we know three or four generations of Milford."

"What are the chances that her killer is still alive?" Abe asks.

"Antoinette was thirty in 1969. If the killer was eighteen or older, we are looking at—arithmetic was not always my strong suit."

"They'd be born from 1951 back," Abe says.

"That's our search parameter," I say.

"That does narrow the list quite a bit," Em says. I can see she has already done the calculation.

Nobody is talking about not learning who the killer was because Antoinette died a half century ago. Everyone is on board, yet we don't know how smooth the sailing will be. The drive to Erin's house is a little over forty-five minutes. Logging trucks and no passing zones slow us down. The hillsides and fields are still snow-covered, and there are large patches of ice forming on the river.

We pull into Erin's driveway just as my in-law, Samantha, pulls in from the other direction. The kiddos come streaming out of the house. You'd think that we haven't seen our grandchildren in years. It goes both ways. I hope that these mutual feelings will last, but I know adorable children turn into teenagers. Erin will have to deal with two girls at various stages of puberty, with Caleb thrown in the middle.

After hugs and stories are shared, we all head inside for a simple lunch of grilled cheese sandwiches or peanut butter and jelly, chips or carrot sticks, and Emelina's cookies. Talk of murder and death is put aside as we focus on the children. Jesse and Caleb have schoolwork to share, and April is not lost for words when showing us her drawings of Chuckles the cat, who has trouble sitting still for her portraits. The cat is nowhere to be found, and Billy knows that upstairs is off limits. Abe and Emelina are not family per se, but they show genuine interest in my extended brood. I have shared much of my life with them since I accepted early retirement. They have heard about my bad times and of times like these. Besides my husband these are the closest people to me. My son Wesley needs his space, and I don't hold it against him.

Just as we get the kids settled with Samantha and Erin describes the process, Ken texts me. *"This was inside the coal furnace."* He attached two photos. One is of a rolled-up rug. The other is of its contents. It took a lot of guts for my husband to take that last photo. I can't imagine how he was feeling.

A second text bings. "The owner is coming over and so are the State Police. Wonder how many more bodies are here?" The next photo is of a skull with a jagged circular hole in the center of the forehead.

Emelina peeks at the photos before I can put my phone away. "Oh my God! Andrew!" she exclaims.

CHAPTER TWELVE

Emelina begins shuddering and shaking like I have never seen her do before. The thought that the other skeleton is her nephew is too much, and she is overcome with grief. Abe holds her tightly while Erin and I circle them both in our arms. A lunch napkin with a smear of jelly on it will have to do until Samantha retrieves a box of tissues. Em ages before our eyes again. Her DNA will prove it soon enough, but in our hearts, we know what happened to Andrew Bidwell. Wife and husband disappeared without a trace fifty years ago, and two sets of remains are found within twenty feet of each other, hidden behind a wall. This is too much of a coincidence. Two homicides. Everything grinds to a halt. We need to tend to the oldest living Bidwell before any talk of how this changes the investigation can be hashed out.

Finally, Emelina comes up for air. "When we learned that Antoinette was murdered, I didn't think for a moment Andrew had anything to do with it. Remember I was there for the three months after she vanished until he disappeared. He was lost without her. He became more and more sure that something bad had happened to her when no one heard from her. We talked about it for hours. He just didn't know what happened or why. He was onto to something, and he died because of it."

Over her shoulder, Erin gives me shrug as if there may be more to Andrew than Emelina's belief in her blood relative. After all, blood is thicker than water.

"For the longest time, I thought the chief of police wanted to arrest Andrew when none of her friends, co-workers, or family heard from her. Andrew was upset about something and was supposed to meet the chief to clear the air. He was never heard from again. Not a word, not a letter, nothing." In the backyard, the snow persons stand silent guard with their backs to Emelina. They have as many answers as we do at this point.

"Let me tell Ken to come here. I don't want him to be alone either," I say. No one argues with me. As much as my man would like to put this all out of his mind, I know he can't keep it bottled up inside. I think that as much for my sake as for his.

I text Ken back that he should come to Erin's home. This time we will offer him comfort and succor and not lay a Joe Friday "just the facts, ma'am, just the facts" on him. After all, he didn't have to send me any of these awful new photos. It was his way of reaching out to us and acknowledging what we were doing today.

When I think for a moment, I realize that I am reeling from the new discovery. More importantly, is this going to kill my oldest and longest friend in Milford? I have never seen her so bereft. Is it better to take her to her doctor for a sedative? Should we take her home? No, it's better that she be here with us. She can lay down in one of the kid's beds. What about Ken, discovering two sets of human remains in less than a week? That is something that no one should have to go through once, let alone twice.

I don't know what I am feeling or thinking now. Part of me is screaming that I should be horrified at what my husband has stumbled into, yet another part of me is trying to make sense of what clues this new discovery affords us. My mind is working like a blender trying to make a smoothie out of blueberries and ball bearings.

Luckily, Abe is getting calmer by the moment. After the shock of the discovery, he is focusing entirely on our friend. "Emelina, dear, we have to breathe. Let's breathe in together and breathe out."

They start, then Erin and I join in. Deep inbreaths and deep outbreaths. Slowly, her sobs become less frequent and less severe. The color returns to her cheeks, and between blowing her nose several times, she gains her composure, then bursts into tears again, so we repeat the process until she is cried out. All the while we focus on our breathing. This process settles my mind as well. I stop the racing thoughts and concentrate on my breath. My body begins to relax. The tension leaves my neck, shoulders, and upper torso. My stomach and bowels are still clenched, and maybe someday I will learn to relax them too. I am positive that is where I bury my deepest feelings.

A voice interrupts my thoughts of white puffy clouds I remember as a little girl lying in the warm grass on a summer's day in the bucolic English countryside.

Abe says, "You are probably right to assume it's Andrew, Em, but there is a small chance it is not. You need to keep that in mind. You don't want to suffer needlessly. We are here for you. How can we help?"

"Abe, just by being here with all of you helps." She looks at Erin and me seated across the table. "What if I was home alone and I got a call from Detective Shafer?" she asks.

None of us wanted to ponder this possibility. We tend to think of our spry elder as always upbeat and curious what the new day will bring to her. I'm afraid that this revelation may be too much for my dearest friend.

She says, "I am better staying here with you. I am not sure I can help much, but I don't want to be alone right now."

Erin and I disengage and move to the kitchen. "How are you feeling, Mommy?" she asks.

"Your father and Emelina's worlds are rocked by this second bunch of bones. Daddy never wanted to see another skeleton again as long as he lived. And Emelina, look at her." I shake my head. "I feel sad for them, but—"

"You are still trying to figure out how the body rolled up in the carpet stuffed in a closed-off coal furnace is connected to the body in the steamer trunk sitting next to it?"

I nod.

"Me, too, but let's help Daddy and Emelina, and then we can sort this out," says the queen of compartmentalization.

"Emelina said something in there that made you shrug. What was that about?"

Erin looks over my shoulder to be sure not to be overhead, then pulls me to the other side of the Bose playing her favorite '90s mix. "What if Andrew strangled Antoinette and hid her body, then killed her lover and put that guy in the furnace?"

"The police chief figured out what happened and called him in, and that's when Andrew decided to flee," I reply, playing Watson to her Holmes.

"Somebody else would have to be reported missing."

"What are the chances of there being record of that from 1970 still kicking around?" I ask.

"Do you think your good friend Officer Barney Williams can look?"

"Maybe. I can ask him."

"Tomorrow?"

"Yes, he will be busy with the second discovery today. The media will explode with this," I say.

"*Historic Mansion, House of Horrors.* I can see the headlines already," she says with a wry smile. Then she asks, "How are you doing?" She is like me when I hear someone deflect the question asked. I will keep repeating the question until they answer it. I didn't answer her and talk about my feelings. I know, I know. I spend too much time in my head, and I don't always check in with my heart. My meditation and yoga practice helps me realize that. When one's mind whirls a mile a minute, it is tough sometimes to ask about those slippery and hard to describe things called feelings. I know where Erin gets her Attention Deficit Disorder from. I could never teach a book class. I needed to be interacting with my students on their level, even if it meant sitting or kneeling on the floor. Being in the moment with those kindergartners all those years forced me to focus on the matter at hand. Rote memorization of multiplication tables? Please. But give me crayons and construction paper, and my students and I could focus for hours.

I found out you could show me crime scene photos and I will ask a question no one else has. That's when Erin said that I had a special gift. So maybe at one time I had the attention span of a five-year-old. I grew out of it, didn't I? I stare at April's drawings of unicorns on the fridge for a long moment and remember that I must answer Erin, who's been waiting during my visit to elsewhere.

"Sad for them, but happy that we may have the answers to where Antoinette and Andrew ended up. I feel sad that two people were killed now, but I think that it will help us solve a half-century old mystery."

"There are other possibilities until we get DNA, but I think it is safe to assume Emelina is right, that her slain kin were hidden in the basement never to be seen or heard from again. We can act on that assumption, but let's not get tunnel vision."

"Agreed."

We return to the dining room to see Abe and Emelina seated side by side on two straight back chairs, silently meditating with closed eyes, hands in a simple mudra position, quietly breathing together in unison. Emelina has a slight smile on her face. Not quite what I was expecting, but Abe has worked his magic on me before. Not to interrupt their flow state, Erin and I head over to the laptops and super-deluxe printer/scanner/everything machine. I begin feeding the beast as she keystrokes bits and bytes into CaseSoft. Everyone needs to be doing what they are doing in this moment.

CHAPTER THIRTEEN

"Officer Williams tells me that you made a request for an archives search of missing persons at or around the time of the disappearance of Andrew and Antoinette Bidwell."

"Your question, Detective Shafer?" I ask.

"I also understand that you and your daughter were at the borough offices when the doors opened this morning to look at the grantor/grantee indexes and building plans and permits for the Devlin mansion.

"That is true." I will make him work for it, I've decided.

"If I didn't know better, I would say that you are conducting a homicide investigation, Mrs. Strong."

Emelina and I are sitting in his office. She has volunteered to give her DNA sample to see if DNA from the coal furnace skeleton matches hers. The air inside is almost as frosty as the winds buffeting the windows of his office overlooking the front parking lot. His short black hair and square chin over a muscular build give him a distinct military bearing. I wonder if he served before joining the State Police. I haven't decided if it is meant to be intimidating. I listen to his even tone and watch his face for any poker tells, then I decide to up the ante.

"I am sure you have your methods, Detective Shafer, but why is it that I was the first to ask for missing persons reports from 1970 and to make a visit to Borough Hall for the Devlin mansion ownership transfers, as well as the first to determine when the conversion from coal to oil took place?" I know something about the timeline, and I am holding off on revealing it to him to see if he will cooperate with us.

"I am not sure that I should be talking with you, Mrs. Strong. Some of the townsfolk have their concerns about your involvement in this matter."

I am taken aback by that. Sure, I know there are a few noses out of joint over my solving the murders of Jake Dawson and Brian Yelito. Detective Shafer had no clue there was a dognapping until after Billy and I found the prize-winning show dog alive and well.

He continues, "The word came down from my superiors to only supply information on a need-to-know basis."

Oafish Barney Williams, in his ill-fitting tight winter uniform, sits uncomfortably off to the side and is smart enough to stay on the sidelines in this battle of wits for which he is unarmed.

Before I can speak, Emelina looks at me, places a gentle hand on my knee, and addresses the man about half my age and a third of hers seated before us.

"With all due respect sir, it seems that Mrs. Strong has accelerated your identification of the bodies by showing me the necklace. If it wasn't for her, you wouldn't have known about my nephew and his wife."

"What makes you think it was your nephew hidden in the furnace?" He is a cool customer and doesn't take the bait.

"We are not sure, Detective Shafer. That is why I asked for the missing persons reports from that time period. Unless the laws of this state have changed, I have a right under the Freedom of Information Act to obtain any and all missing person records from that time period. Until you test that DNA sample," I say, pointing to the test kit on his desk, "we won't know for sure."

"Certainly, information from the public is always welcome," he says diplomatically.

"Has she done anything to upset your apple cart?" Emelina asks politely, but there is an edge to her piercing glare at Shafer.

"We welc—" Shafer starts, but Emelina interrupts him.

"Seems like Gwendolyn is supplying you with all the pieces of your puzzle."

"There's no deny—"

"And if you show her a few of your pieces, it seems to me that she can fit in some more."

"We are perfectly capable—"

"Maybe this is a good time for Officer Williams to show an elderly woman to the lady's room and let you two have a chance to talk off the record." With that, she stands up. "Officer Williams?"

Barney looks at Shafer, then at Emelina and finally at me. I shrug.

"No problem, Ms. Bidwell. Can I get you a soda while we are out there?" my former student asks. He always had good manners.

Em looks at Shafer. "And some crackers too. My stomach is upset with all this talk of murder."

The door closes after they leave. I hope Shafer will show his hand. I am holding an ace and I know it.

He starts. "The mayor is getting heat from Truscott Daniels and Mike Meade. He called my troop commander."

"Daniels, the trust attorney in town?" I ask. He nods. "Mike Meade sits on the Bloodstone Museum board and is the father of my nemesis, Mary Meade, the school superintendent." Both of them are old enough to swim in the suspect pool.

"Two for two."

"Why would two of the town's most prominent persons want me to stand down?"

"I asked myself that same question, Mrs. Strong. If these were recent murders, I would say that they'd be trying to cover for the suspects. My commander told me they said dredging up the past would be bad for the town. People would not want to come here to work or live here if it had a bad reputation."

"He didn't ask you to stand down, I hope."

"No, but the message was clear. I have to tread lightly."

"Nobody was supposed to break down the divider in the Delvin basement." I think of my poor husband, who should probably see a therapist after what he has been through.

"Nobody was supposed to know about where Andrew and Antoinette ended up," Shafer hypothesizes. "They just got fed up with living in this Podunk town and were never heard from again."

"Podunk town?" I ask without being offended.

"One guy is known for handling the big trusts in town, and the other guy sits on a museum board. Excuse my French, Mrs. Strong, but they don't give a rat's patootie about the future. They are all about preserving the past and the wishes of Milford's wealthiest patrons."

Until now, I hadn't considered my young colleague in crime detection to be a big-picture thinker, and he instantly earns more respect. I know he has to navigate tricky currents and I don't. I know that getting a fifty-year-old murder dumped on his desk is not his idea of a fun time. Now he has two, and with that, his investigation is going to be put under the microscope. On top of that, I am a wildcard that he must deal with.

"Mark, I know which came first."

He is startled by my use of his first name. "What are you talking about?"

"You know, that chicken or the egg thing. I know which came

first." I lay down my ace. "T.J. Mardell was the owner of the Devlin Mansion when this all took place."

I show him a copy of the photocopy from the land records book showing the property transfer. "He converted the heating system to oil in the spring of 1970, then the building inspector signed off on the permit on May 12, 1970. It was a Tuesday." I lay that sheet of paper down next.

"Okay," he says.

"What date was the last day of any of the newspapers in the steamer trunk?"

I see the lightbulb go on. "June something."

"June 23rd." I show him a picture on my phone.

He starts to connect the dots. "The coal furnace could have been disconnected during the warmer weather of the spring but was probably not functioning when the oil heater took over. The body could have been dumped in the furnace before May 12th."

"Andrew disappeared on March 31st," I say.

"And somebody fills the steamer trunk with drapes and newspapers in June or later," he adds.

He's quick. He continues, "Even though the body in the furnace was discovered after the body in the steamer trunk, the furnace was filled first and then the steamer trunk went into the basement next." He stops to digest that. "When was the wall built separating the basement?"

"Ken tells me that it was cosmetic. It had no structural purpose. I don't know yet."

I bring out another piece of paper. "Here is Mardell's obituary." I lay that on top of the other gifts I am giving to Shafer.

"Damn," he says.

"Here are the names, addresses, and telephone numbers of his surviving children." I let him absorb that for a couple of beats. "Did you ever play in the basement or attic of your parent's house?" I ask.

He looks at me with a furrowed brow. "Why are you giving me these leads? Why don't you want to work them yourself?"

"They are all out of towners. They might remember Emelina, but I didn't come into town until 1985. Who would be better to call them up? The detective investigating two bodies found in their family home, or a former kindergarten teacher nosing around? Who is going to get a better version of the truth?"

Emelina returns to the office. Before Barney's bulk shadows the doorframe, Shafer slides the paper I gave him into his file.

Shafer stands and comes around from behind his desk. "Thank you for coming in, Ms. Bidwell. We will be in touch." He extends a hand to me, and I shake it. "Once again, Mrs. Strong, it is a pleasure seeing you."

The rules of engagement are established. I have to give a little to get a little. He has done me a favor and warned me to watch my back.

"We can see ourselves out." Emelina says.

My mentor and I walk through the maze of halls to the front doors and out to my car. We are going to Erin's house again and will meet Abe there. There is a lot of work still to do.

"Did Detective Shafer warm up at all?" she asks me.

I give a distracted nod to her question. "Yes. He told me who's been raising concerns about me—Truscott Daniels and Mike Meade. They are old enough to be the killers, but what motive would they have? By coming forward, they attract attention to themselves. I have to suppose they are trying to keep reputations unsullied. I am the wildcard they can't control, but they can try to control the flow of information between Shafer and myself." The tightness in my chest is warning me, but I am not sure why.

"You know what that tells you, Gwendolyn."

"What?"

"Some important people are afraid you might figure this out."

I nod as my mind whirls a mile a minute. Politicians and the town's movers and shakers want me to stand down. This is not like arguing with a school principal about some idiotic policy. These people play hardball.

She smiles and looks over to me. "You go, girl."

I return my best fake smile.

CHAPTER FOURTEEN

"Daniels and Meade can go jump in the river," I say to Abe and Erin. My soup sits untouched on Erin's dining room table as I stew over what Shafer told me. Teaching in a school system where I had no desire for advancement gave me plenty of opportunities to display righteous anger. Those muscles got a regular workout. "Who do they think they are, going through back channels to the State Police, telling him not to talk with me?"

The heat in my belly is familiar from those times the school principals would try to sell me on some stupid policies contrary to the welfare of the children. I had a simple guiding North Star: I'd ask, "How does this help my students?" The revolving door of principals who came and went at Milford Elementary learned very quickly that Mrs. Strong was not somebody to play with. Then there were those situations where I would be called into the office to explain what I was doing with an injured baby rabbit or robin in the classroom. To this day, I still have former students or their parents stop me in the grocery store to tell me how they remembered the bunny or bird we nursed to health.

I could get my hackles up, and I wouldn't back down at some of the bureaucratic BS passed down to the teachers. Ken would have to help me down from the ceiling when I had to deal with school administrators who never sat on the floor of a classroom and wiped a runny nose. Meade's daughter was one of those bureaucrats who delighted in wielding her power. So, by kinship, her father was already on my short list.

"That's how politics work, Gwen," Abe says. "By going through the mayor, they have plausible deniability. They will act offended if you call them on it."

"Mom, Emelina is correct in saying they are afraid what you might find. You are a force of nature," Erin tells me. "Figure out what they are trying to protect, and that will help us with narrowing down who killed Antoinette and Andrew."

We are on a first-name basis describing the victims. Emelina made sure to tell us everything she could remember about both. The newspaper stories helped jog her memory. Erin added notes to the documents that Abe and I scanned into CaseSoft. Emelina has made that turbulent period of history come alive for us. It was a time when Johnny Cash and Jimi Hendrix were playing back-to-back on the same AM radio station. Bell bottom jeans, halter tops, mini-skirts, and go-go boots competed with vested suits, mink stoles, and evening dresses.

"Tell me, is it better for the town to leave two murders unsolved than to try to figure out who killed them?" I shake my head.

"Not for the town's upper crust," Emelina said. "Back then, you still had vestiges of the landed gentry looking aghast at their workers with their free love, drugs, and rock and roll. I had one foot in both worlds. My father married my mother for love and turned his back on the snobbery of his wealthy family. I was fortunate that my great grandmother saw something in me and made it possible for me to attend a teacher's college during the second world war."

"Then you taught kindergarten for forty years until I came

along," I say. A younger version of me said she was old then. I swear she hasn't changed a bit since I met her.

"I knew the day I met you that you would take care of the children. That is when I planned my retirement."

"I was this scared mixed-race kid who fell in love with teaching kindergarten, and I have you to thank for it, Emelina," I tell her. Then my phone rings.

"Hello?"

"Hi, Mrs. Strong, this is Vickie Scudder at the police department. I had to go into the basement and look at old index cards in the filing drawers for your Freedom of Information request. I couldn't find any reports from back them, but I have two index cards. One for Antoinette Bidwell and the other for a Jeremy Webster."

My heart hammers. "When did Webster go missing?"

"It looks like October 23rd, 1970."

I say out loud, "Jeremy Webster, missing October 23rd, 1970. What was his date of birth?"

"November 27th, 1954."

"November 27th, 1954," I repeat.

Abe shakes his head and says softly. "He was not quite sixteen when he went missing."

Erin is on it in a flash.

"Who was the officer who took the report of Antoinette?" I ask.

"Officer Timothy Sweet."

Erin shakes her head and says, "Webster is alive and well living in Flagstaff, Arizona."

"Thank you, Vickie," I say.

"There's two other things I need to tell you, Mrs. Strong."

"What's that, dear?"

"Barney and that detective were over at the town clerk's office and the building department. They were looking at who owned that old house and what work was done on it."

It figures that Shafer wants to get his own copies of the paperwork I gave him. A newly learned phrase, "plausible deniability," enters my mind. "What was the other thing, Vickie?"

"I was told to only give these to Barney. That order came right from my father."

"I see." Vickie's father is the mayor.

"I am calling you from the bathroom. I can't make you copies. I am afraid that Barney will tell you there are no reports, which is technically true, but I figured there may be something important on the index cards."

"Thank you, Vickie."

"Find out who killed those poor people, Mrs. Strong," she says.

"I'll do my best."

"Gotta go." She ends the call.

"This is Timothy Sweet," Abe says, holding up a photocopy we made at the library. He lays it on the table for all of us to view. "He is shaking hands with Herman Kenrick, Milford's chief of police."

"The caption says that Sweet is the newest police officer to join the force. The photo was taken in February of 1968," Abe adds.

"That makes sense," Erin says. "The new guy on the force would get stuck working a midnighter on Christmas Eve."

Emelina shakes her head. "I don't remember him."

"His name appears a few more times in the local papers into 1970 and then no more," Erin reads from her computer screen.

"Wonder what happened to him?" I ask.

"The pay for police and teachers was very low back then. If he had a family or wanted to plan one, he may have gone into another line of work," Emelina says.

We finish eating, and my adorable grandchildren go down for their nap. There will be two hours of quiet before Erin and I play with them before dinner. We head over to her office, and she uncaps an erasable marker. "What have we learned? Phrase it as a question."

"How did the order of how they got into the basement change things?" Abe says.

We all sit with that for a moment. Better to think on it than blurt out a fast answer.

"How long was Antoinette alive before she was placed in the trunk?" Erin asks. She's writing down all of our questions, including her own.

"Were the drapes from the Devlin Mansion or somewhere else?" I ask.

"Why leave an old coal furnace in your basement? Wouldn't you want to remove it when you installed the oil burner?" Abe asks.

"When did the partition go up?" Erin asks.

"She was strangled, and he was shot," I add. I almost forget to phrase it as a question. "Why is that important?"

"Who installed the oil burner?" Emelina asks.

"Who was the actual building inspector who signed off on the permit?" Erin asks.

The whiteboard is filling up quickly.

"Once the wall went up, was there a way to get the trunk in the basement?" Abe asks.

"Did T.J. Mardell know what was happening?" I ask.

When there are no more offerings, Erin says, "Let's tackle them in reverse order. His children were not teenagers yet. Would he want them to discover what was in the steamer trunk?"

"That's why the partition went up," I say. "If you weren't hiding bodies in the basement, you could have left the entire basement open."

Erin says, "What if you are installing the oil burner and see this as a way to dispose of Andrew and Antoinette?"

"You tell Devlin that the coal furnace is too big or bulky to remove, so you offer to hide it behind a wall. You slip the trunk in and drag the carpet containing Andrew when no one is looking," Abe says, answering two of our questions with one answer.

"Ken said that the wall was cheap and easy to build, just slapping paneling on two-by-four framing," I add.

"Disable the coal furnace. Drop the body into the furnace, drag the steamer trunk in, and wall it all off," Erin says.

"It would take two strong men," Abe points out.

"What do you mean, Abe?" Emelina asks.

"Lifting a full-grown man wrapped in a carpet to the flue opening of the furnace would take two men. Also, carrying the steamer trunk that size requires two people, especially going down basement stairs."

"So, the killer had help," Erin concludes.

"How do we know it was just one killer?" I ask.

"Right," Abe says. "One was strangled, and the other was shot."

"Was one a crime of passion and the other an execution?" I ask.

"What are you thinking, Gwendolyn?" Emelina asks.

The words spew out before my brain fully forms the thought. "Antoinette went out Christmas Eve to buy a last-minute present and never returned. Over six months later, her body was folded into the trunk with newspapers from the summertime. Was she lured to her death? This was not a random killing, especially with her husband being discovered with a bullet hole in his head."

"Why not shoot her?" Abe asks.

"It would make her death pre-meditated," Erin says. "If I understand my mom correctly, she is asking if Antoinette's murder was a crime of passion. The killer was presented with a decision…"

"What did we learn at the crime symposium, Erin?" I then answer my own question. "The opportunity and motive became apparent to the killer, but the only means the killer had was to—"

"Squeeze her neck with such force as to fracture a bone in her throat," Erin finishes my line of reasoning.

"That makes it a crime of passion," Abe said.

Erin and I nod.

"Shooting my nephew was planned," Emelina says. "He started to put things together at about the time he told me the chief of police was considering him as a suspect, and that is when he was killed."

We all look at Emelina, and I realize that I am not the only kindergarten teacher in the room. She's had nearly a century to study human nature and taught me everything I knew.

"Since his death was planned, the killer had time to think of how he would dispose of the body. The coal furnace came to mind," I say.

"Place the steamer trunk in the basement and partition it off," Erin says.

"Andrew's death makes keeping Antoinette alive for any period of time after she disappeared questionable. She was killed Christmas Eve and kept somewhere until the idea of putting her in the trunk in the basement was formulated." No one knocks my theory down.

We look at the questions still left on the board. Abe says, "T.J. Mardell wouldn't be stupid enough to use one of his own steamer trunks. I think he is unaware of the whole scheme. The work in the basement presented the killer with an opportunity to dispose of both bodies."

Scanning the board, we are left with four important questions. Who installed the oil burner? Did they also erect the partition?

Where did the drapes come from? Can we still talk to former officer Timothy Sweet?

Erin says, "I am going to call Daddy."

Before I can object, I hear, "Hi Daddy, would you know who installed the oil burner in the Devlin mansion?" A pause. "I see." A longer pause. "That's terrible." Erin shakes her head at us. I fear more bad news. "Okay, I'll be sure to tell Mom."

I look at her as she ends the call. My no-nonsense daughter is not known for diplomacy, but I can see she is trying form the words. Her head bounces back and forth.

"What?" I ask.

She blurts out, "Daddy's been fired by the doctor who owns the mansion. The police escorted him while he got his tools out. He was told you were spreading rumors around town and showing people the photographs taken of the skeletons."

CHAPTER FIFTEEN

"You can't go in there, Mrs. Strong. He's in a meeting."

"Thank you, Allison," I say to my former student, a paralegal for Truscott Daniels.

I have never been in his office before, but as I turn the handle to the massive dark-stained oak door and walk in, I am not the least concerned with propriety. He's messing with my husband's income.

Across from him sits Michael Meade. I see that I am not dressed in my Sunday best for this intrusion. I don't own a power suit. Daniels is wearing his, a perfectly tailored charcoal-gray business suit that is just a shade darker than his silvery hair. A recent vacation to a warm weather location adds color to his handsome face. He bolts to a standing position. An older Mike Meade, wearing a navy-blue blazer, red power tie over starched white shirt, and gray trousers, jerks to his feet a beat later in response to Daniel's movements. I stride in purposefully. I am wearing a white parka over beige wool sweater and jeans. My duck shoes complete my winter walking attire. I plant myself on his Persian rug, equidistant from both men.

"Exactly what is your problem with me, boys?" As Meade

backs up to the window overlooking Milford's main thoroughfare, I close the distance to keep the triangle perfect. The window is two stories above the pavement. It is not a wise escape route.

"Mrs. Strong, you have no business here," Daniels snaps at me. "Please leave."

"Not until you tell me why the mayor carried your complaints to the State Police and why my husband had to be removed from the Devlin mansion renovation." I am not practiced at glaring at people, but a righteous anger is simmering inside, and I give them my best tight-lipped, steely-eye squint. Am I really standing here with clenched fists on my hips ready to give them a blast?

"Allison," Daniels says loudly, "please escort Mrs. Strong out my office."

I turn to see an anxious Allison torn between her employer and her former kindergarten teacher. "You don't need anybody else to do your dirty work, Truscott," I say. "You owe me an explanation, and I am not leaving here until I get it."

"Mrs. Strong, there must be some misunderstand—"

I glare at Meade. "Don't hand me that crap, Michael. I understand perfectly well what you are doing. Why do you both want to stop me from helping Emelina Bidwell look into the murders of her nephew and his wife?"

Reddening above the collar, Daniels says, "Your irresponsible actions are bringing unfavorable attention to the town. The mayor made that known to the State Police."

"If something wasn't done, those pictures your husband took would be all over the internet," Meade adds, mustering some false courage to add legitimacy to his colleague's assertions.

I open my mouth to retort, but my attention is drawn to an undated black and white framed photo of Milford's movers and shakers wearing tuxedos at some gala event. In it, a very young Truscott Daniels stands next to a man I recognize from some of the newspaper articles we gathered at the library. I now split the distance between the two men and lean against the corner of the desk to get a better look. "When was this photo taken?" I ask Daniels in a softer voice.

"It had to be the early 1970s," he says before he realizes the importance of his answer. So unlawyerly.

"Shortly after they disappeared," I murmur.

Both men are looking at me as I retreat a few steps.

The photo raises an important question. "Save me the trouble of going to the probate court. Who is the lawyer handling the Bloodstone Family Trust?"

"I will do no such thing, Mrs. Strong. Now if you don't want me to call the police, I'll kindly ask you to leave for the last time."

I step back to the doorway. My mind is taking in the new information I just received. If I hadn't barged into their inner sanctum, I never would have gotten one of the answers I was looking for.

"Thank you, gentlemen. I understand now why it is so important to stop drawing attention to the murders of Antoinette and Andrew Bidwell. There is one more thing. The Stillman brothers have agreed to fund my big-city lawyer in suing you both for unfair restraint of trade should my husband lose another account."

"Are you threatening me, Mrs. Strong?" Daniels stammers.

"You come after me or my family again and you will find out exactly what I am capable of. Good day, gentlemen." I march out of the office, pulling the door shut a little louder than I wanted to, then stop at Allison's desk. The slamming reverberates up my hand to my elbow.

"Sorry, Allison. I don't like it when grown men pee in the sandbox."

"I can't believe you did that." Ken is trying to suppress a smile after I recount my brief meeting with two of the town's power players.

"If it was me they were messing with, you would have done the same thing."

"The only difference is that they would have called the police on me after an ambulance was called. Do you know a good bail bondsman?"

I smile. "I know some people who do."

Lunch at home with Ken on a workday is a rarity. Billy is watching Ken's every movement on the odd chance that he will drop a tasty morsel or get up from his seat. The pooch has been known to run off with a half-eaten sandwich.

We are not going to let the bigshots get away with any shenanigans. Our differences over Ken's discoveries in the basement are set aside now that we have a common foe.

"I can't stop wondering what the connection between Mardell and the Bloodstone family is," I say.

"He owned a car dealership, and they were the leading industrialists at the time. One hand washes the other," Ken replies. "I'd like to know who built the partition. I see a lot of rusty oil burners sitting next to new gas furnaces. People will drain the oil tanks to prevent a leak or a spill, but they don't haul them away."

"Have you ever seen someone partition off a basement?" I ask.

"Plenty of times, for extra storage space or to make an additional bedroom. Milford has quite a few legal apartments in the basements of some of the oldest Victorian homes."

"Isn't that against code?" I ask.

"Not if the homeowner lives in that space. As long as they don't rent it out, they are fine. I've built plenty of kitchenettes and showers below ground. The landlords live in the basement and rent out the upper floors."

"But what about just separating the mechanicals, like what you found there?"

"Never. That's why I'd like to know who built the partition," he says. "It was done cheap; I don't think it was a contractor. It could be done in a day by two people."

I think of what Abe said that two people were needed to move the steamer trunk and the rolled-up carpet.

"Do you think it was done to hide what you found?" I know I am asking him to relive the trauma at the house of horrors.

"The more I think about it, the more I am convinced that they built the wall to hide the bodies."

"How do you sell that idea to the owner of the house?"

"Not that I would do it," Ken says, "but the reasoning would follow like this." He stops to compose his speech. "Mr. or Mrs. Homeowner, you don't want any future buyers to ask if there is asbestos in that coal furnace. I can erect a fake wall to hide them, and nobody has to be the wiser. It will be cheaper for me to build the wall than to break it up and haul it away. People will think they are buying a house with just the oil burner and tank, totally oblivious to the monstrous cast iron coal burner behind the wall."

"What kind of conversation did you and the good doctor have about the basement?" I ask.

"He wanted to restore the building to the time it was built. The original building plans showed much more space in the basement than what we found down there. It ran the full length and width of the upstairs floors. I peeled back a sheet of plywood and discovered the coal furnace, coal chute, and bin. Since he was planning to go completely solar, everything had to be removed. Because the mansion was added to the Historical Registry years before he bought it, they would only allow him to make restorations as part of his purchase agreement. He was able to get tax credits by adding the solar. The Historical Registry allowed the exemption as long as the solar panels couldn't be seen from the street. The rear roof had southern exposure, so it was a perfect plan."

"Now it's a haunted house," I say.

"I am sure the seller had no clue when they sold it to him."

"Or did they?"

"I doubt it. When I busted down the walls, there was a thick layer of dust on top of the coal dust. The cobwebs hung from every joist. Nobody had been back there since the wall went up."

"Do you think the wall builder knew what was back there?" This was a question that was already discussed at Erin's house, but I welcome his opinion. My husband isn't an amateur sleuth and doesn't play one on TV. But he knows buildings and home remodeling.

I know where Erin learned to bounce her head back and forth sideways as he weighs his thoughts. He finally says, "Does a bear go poopie in the woods?"

"Speaking of that subject, do you want to take Billy for a walk, since you have the afternoon off? I want to update Emelina," I say.

"How about we both go? The three of us go around town and show them we are together in this."

I love this man.

CHAPTER SIXTEEN

We bundle up and head out, Billy leading the way to Emelina's cottage. Recent days of bright sun and temperatures above freezing have made the sidewalks slippery, then overnight the snowmelt has frozen into treacherous black ice. We slip-slide the few blocks to her cottage. Both of us always lived within walking distance of the now-shuttered Milford Elementary. I knew I could always count on her during times when I had nobody to talk to about a problem with a student, or more often, issues with school administrators.

I had stopped on my way home from Daniel's office to confirm at the probate court that Truscott Daniels set up the Bloodstone Family Trust. I was told that a trust is a mechanism for wealth preservation and minimizing tax consequences for large sums being handed down to future generations. It is incumbent upon the trustee to carry out the expressed wishes of the trust. Benjamin Bloodstone holds the title of trustee. The Bloodstone Family Trust had their fingerprints on almost every philanthropic endeavor for as long as I've lived in Milford. Benjamin likes to work behind the scenes and does not seek the limelight.

We turn the corner and see a familiar sedan next to Emelina's ancient Mercury.

"She has company," Ken says.

We pick up our pace, and Billy senses that the hunt is on. Detective Shafer's car hood is warm to the touch. He hasn't been here long. I don't always pick up on phone calls or text messages when I am out walking Billy. It's not because I ignore them. It's because I keep my phone on vibrate and don't always feel it when my little canine buddy pulls me briskly around town. I grab my phone and see a text from Emelina. *Detective Shafer is here at my house, come quick.*

We stamp our feet on her porch, then Ken knocks on her front door. She peeks through the parlor window and opens the door. "What a nice surprise. I was just offering Detective Shafer some tea and cookies."

Ken and the detective make eye contact. "You are about to have a real treat, sir. Emelina makes the best cookies in the county," he says.

I realize that Ken and Shafer have met a couple of times now while standing over the dead. I help her with the tea service while she hands him a warm snickerdoodle on a napkin.

"Do you take your tea with milk or sugar?" I ask Shafer.

"Just honey," he says. Milford has a few wonderful apiaries producing the best honey. We all buy local and eschew the store brands. One apiary has its own 24/7 livestream. I get mesmerized watching the beekeeper use the smoker around the hive. That's good entertainment.

Shafer pours a teaspoon of liquid goodness onto his spoon and swirls it in his fine china cup.

Balancing the snickerdoodle on his knee, he sips the tea and closes his eyes. Next, he balances the saucer and cup on his other knee and pops the tasty treat into his mouth. He repeats the closed eyes routine while he chews slowly. I keep Billy on his leash.

Snickerdoodles resting on knees around the living room can be too tempting for him.

We sip and chew expecting the explanation from Shafer for his unannounced visit to her home.

Finally, he clears his voice. "I appreciate your hospitality, Ms. Bidwell. I came by today because I have some news. I did not think it was appropriate to call you on the phone. The DNA tests came back last evening. The tests were expedited when Mr. Strong found the carpet in the coal furnace." He is being discreet with Emelina. He looks over to me and returns his gaze to her. "Unfortunately, you were correct. The bodies in the Devlin mansion are of your nephew and his wife. I wanted to tell you first before we released this information to the public."

"Thank you for your kindness, Detective Shafer. Will I be able to start the funeral process for them?" Emelina is not surprised by this news and seems ready to take the next steps in her grieving process.

"Doctor Cleary has the final say, but I think you can make arrangements with the funeral home for the pick-up and transfer." He sips his tea. "We are treating both deaths as homicides, and I will continue consulting with cold case experts."

"I don't think you will have any more interference from Truscott Daniels and Mike Meade," I say. "I made it clear to them this morning I won't tolerate their interference in Ken's ability to earn an income. I got their attention."

"I'm sure you did, Mrs. Strong. I am sure you did."

"Care for another cookie, Detective?" Emelina asks.

He nods.

"Have two," she says.

He doesn't protest and places one on his saucer while holding the other in his hand. "It was a good thing you called us before you carted away the furnace, Mr. Strong. We were able to find the cause of death for Mr. Bidwell."

"Did enough of the bullet survive to be able to determine its caliber?" I ask.

"Mrs. Strong, you continue to amaze me. I cannot confirm or deny the presence of a 158-gram .38 caliber slug found in excellent condition in the bottom of the furnace." He talks as if he is just discussing baseball scores. I realize which cold case experts he is consulting with now. Now it's my turn.

"If you visit Truscott Daniels in his offices, you will find an old photo on the wall of him standing next to Burgess Bloodstone. Michael Meade was in the same photo. Daniels' law firm handles the Bloodstone Family Trust, and Meade is the executive director of the board overseeing the Bloodstone Museum of Commerce and Industry," I say.

"I see," he says.

"The photo was from the time period in question. He could tell you who all the movers and shakers were back in the day. It would save you a ton of time," I say.

Almost on cue, Emelina says. "T.J. Mardell was new money back then. He had one of the first Japanese car dealerships in town. He wanted so badly to be accepted by the rich and powerful folks. He tried cozying up to them at the country club and at charity events. He thought that by buying the Devlin Mansion and fixing it up, it would make him one of them."

"You have to wonder what other favors he would do for them," Ken says nonchalantly while petting our doggie. "As a remodeler, I can only think of one reason for that partition."

Shafer enjoys the cookies, tea, and intel in equal measures. The last cookie leaves a little sugar on his lips. He finishes the tea and swipes the crumbs from his slacks before standing. "I will keep you apprised of any developments. It's been fifty years since they were killed, but I promised you I would do my best, and I will."

He nods to all of us and lets Billy sniff his hand before he pets him on the head. We are all good with this exchange.

His V-8 rumbles to life and the gravel crunches under his wheels to signal his departure.

"Sorry, I didn't get your message right away, but we were on our way over here anyway," I say to Emelina.

She turns to me. "Deep in my heart, I was hoping that the person wearing my niece's necklace wasn't her and that somebody else was rolled up in that carpet."

"By coming forward as you did, Emelina, the police have identified them quickly and can get started on finding their killers," Ken says.

"I have to plan two funerals, so I may not be able to help much," she says.

"*We* have two funerals to plan, Emelina. You are not alone." I get up from the couch, cross the room, and lift her from her favorite chair into my arms. Ken and Billy stand as silent witnesses to our bond.

"Detective Shafer told you about the slug they found at the bottom of the coal furnace?" Erin asks me.

My adorable grandchildren are in bed and Erin is getting ready for her work as a civilian contractor to the FBI. We use this window of time to catch up. We use an app where we can see each other and share screens on our laptops. "Yes, and I reciprocated with him about how Meade and Daniels are connected to the Bloodstones. What is their professional interest in two murders from five decades ago?"

"I think we should explore that connection and see how it bears on Antoinette," she says.

"I agree, but why only Antoinette?"

"We can assume that Andrew was killed when he started to suspect what happened to her. Find her killer, and that will lead us to his."

"I see your logic. Still don't know why she was killed, though."

"It doesn't have to be complicated. The more we learn about Antoinette and who was in her circle of acquaintances, the better idea we will have about her life and why someone felt the need to end it."

"I'll be busy for the next several days helping Emelina with funeral arrangements," I tell her.

"That's okay. I will keep you posted in CaseSoft. We learned about many people for that time period from the telephone directory, newspaper accounts, and yearbooks. I have to run them through all the online newspaper archives and social media aggregators. That will take time. Let's figure out who is alive and who can we talk to."

"Sounds like a plan," I say.

"You don't sound so certain, Mom."

"Fifty years is a long time, honey."

"Yeah, but look how you have already poked a few bears. Watch and see."

"Just having those two guys wanting to slow us down gives me enough motivation to see this thing through to the end. Telling me that I have no business looking into the deaths of my best friend's family members and threatening your father's business are enough to light my fire."

She gets busy sharing a screen with me. This time it's The Doors' "Light My Fire" video.

I love this girl.

CHAPTER SEVENTEEN

Several days pass. Erin updates me regularly. There has been no word from Shafer. I wasn't expecting anyone to walk into his offices and confess. Yoga, meditation, and long walks allow me to concentrate on the double homicides from years gone by. I work tirelessly with Emelina on the hundred and one little things that need to be done for the funerals. Today, the images of the skeletons on the dusty mansion floor give way to more acceptable ones. I stare at two polished silver urns in front of a decent gathering in Milford's largest funeral home. Doc Cleary had given permission for the cremations after the skeletal remains of both Mr. and Mrs. Bidwell were identified by DNA.

Stands of flowers from the Chamber of Commerce and other civic organizations flank the urns. Their colors and scents make for a warm contrast to the gloom outside and the subdued drapery of the main viewing room. Soft organ music is piped in through speakers in each corner.

I sit next to Emelina, who is the only Bidwell family member present. Abe sits next to her on the other side, and my family sits behind us. She has outlived all her kin. Elderly Sorrento cousins from out of town and their children come to pay their respects to

Antoinette, who has been missing from their lives for over half a century. It's an act of familial obligation that Emelina appreciates.

Unmarried and childless, Emelina fawned over her niece, and she appreciates the outpouring of condolences on this damp, bone-chilling February day. Foul play was not suspected when Antoinette disappeared, but then everyone had thought Andrew skipped town when the police started looking at him as a suspect. It was then when people began wondering what happened to her. The sheer number of years of not hearing from either of them left a hole in Emelina's heart. It is now filling with grief and maybe something else, but I can't put my finger on it. I must admit that over the years I have known her, I was the one needing her wisdom and solace. My stepmother, Jean, and my father were there for me when it involved anything to do with my kids, but Emelina was there for all the issues of being a kindergarten teacher. As budgets shrunk and the state mandated all forms of testing, I needed her desperately as a sane sounding board.

I can only think of a handful of times when I could help her on some matter. Feisty and independent, Emelina Bidwell made it clear that she could take care of herself. She never seemed to age. Her indomitable spirit and infectious good cheer were the outpouring of her energy to live life even more fully after her retirement from teaching. Since discovering her niece's death, I have seen Em's pain transform her into a tired old woman whose better years are behind her. I am hoping that after today, we can help restore her liveliness and spunk.

We know most, if not all, the folks who have gathered. I am reminded that we didn't get Benjamin Bloodstone's order and I will talk to him after the service. We are a week away from the party and need to get all our supplies. He sits with Truscott Daniels and Michael Meade across the aisle and immediately behind the Sorrento family representatives.

The non-denominational speaker, a chaplain from the hospital, does an excellent job of bringing to life both Andrew and Antoinette. My eyes are drawn to their wedding album photos resting on pedestals in front of the urns as she speaks. The smiles of the happy couple remind me that they were lovers and real people, not just two skeletons found in a basement.

I half-expected to see Detective Shafer, but instead only Barney Williams sits to the rear. We make eye contact. Somebody should teach that man how to dress. I haven't decided whether I want to tweak him about the index cards Vickie found in the moldy basement of Borough Hall. There will be other reasons to visit him, I am sure. I can be sure that the police investigation is plodding along at a far slower pace than ours. They have yet to visit the library for the yearbooks, Cole Directories, and newspaper reels. We have not heard through the small-town grapevine of any interviews being conducted. I am sure I will be the first to talk to many people still alive from the time the Bidwells disappeared.

Looking around, I doubt the killer or killers are here, but then again, I am reminded by the Nazi war criminals who were tracked down, living quiet unassuming lives decades after they stood erect in their black uniforms staring into the camera with soulless eyes. The attendees here today with their walkers and canes outnumber the able-bodied by a serious margin.

Meade and Daniels look uncomfortable sitting next to Bloodstone. Did he drag them here? There is no mention of strangulation or a shooting death, no salacious tidbits for the press to sensationalize Milford like in *The Amityville Horror*. The way they acted around Benjamin before we all sat down for the service reminds me of how one keeps an eye on the crazy uncle. It is like they are his minders. I've known him for all the time I have been in town, and he is one of the nicest people I know, always willing to help organize a charity for a good cause. He is more than the president of the Chamber of Commerce; he is their Goodwill ambassador. Through the decades, he could match Emelina for energy and optimism, but today he too looks drawn and tired. Is it the weather?

Benjamin is taking in every word of the eulogies. I watch his eyes focus on the wedding album photos. I quickly do the math and figure that he was younger than Andrew by a decade. Did he even know them? He would have been a late teenager or just out of college.

Ken sits to my other side. I squeeze his hand. He is here for me and Emelina. Since the two suits across the aisle got him kicked off the restoration project, he has decided to not be an impediment to my snooping around. I will remain careful discussing the case in front of him, but at least he is accepting of my role in helping Emelina get closure. His work has picked back up, and if he never walks back into the Devlin mansion again, he will be just fine with that. He knows the contractor that the new owner hired and figures that he will get a call to work on the upper floors after the owner sees the difference in quality and pricing.

There is no gathering planned for after the service, so the funeral director thanks everyone for attending and reminds everyone to sign the attendance book before departing. Emelina remains seated as the people say their goodbyes to her. Benjamin is behind her, studying the wedding photos with keen interest.

I make my way to him. "Did you know them, Benjamin?"

I startle him. He blinks away tears and says, "A little. I am sad for Emelina. To find out after all these years that they met such a terrible ending must be really hard for her."

"She has her bad days and her good days," I say.

Bloodstone doesn't take his eyes off the photos. "I would see Antoinette at the library occasionally checking out books. She was such a dreamer. I knew Andrew from business associations at the Chamber and Rotary. I was very young then. I had gone away to college and graduate school. The town changed so much while I was away, but not everything."

"How so?" I ask.

Glancing over at Daniels and Meade, he says. "Some people didn't like change. They wanted things to stay the way it was. I was exposed to many different viewpoints while I was away at school, and coming home was like stepping back into the 1950s."

"Was it the war?"

"Partly, but also the movement of jobs down South and to Mexico. My father railed at it all. I remember him rolling down the windows of his Cadillac to curse at the hippies when he veered the car towards them in town." Ben shakes his head at the memories.

The crowd around Emelina thins out. My family stands in the back of the room waiting for me. Ben walks over to her and says, "Again, I am sorry for your loss. I will call upon you in the next couple of days if that is alright." He touches her hand and glances once more at the photos before taking a different exit from the room.

"Are you going to be okay?" I ask Emelina.

She nods.

"I'll be sure she gets home," Abe says.

Em stands and shrugs off Abe's hand on her shoulder, saying, "We have work to do. What time would be good for you, Gwendolyn?"

"I didn't ask Benjamin about the cookie order. He seemed rather preoccupied."

"I wasn't talking about the cookies, dear. When can Abe and I sit down with you and Erin? We have unfinished business. I want to know what happened to them." Her eyes blaze with a fierceness I've only seen a few times over the years when the school board tried to pull a fast one. The woman I had just observed sitting in exhausted grief was now buzzing with a determined energy. She points to the urns. "I won't bury them until we know what happened. They will not be laid to rest until I know, Gwen. Do you understand that?"

"Let me check with Erin." I walk quickly back to her and whisper in her ear. Erin holds up her hand to Emelina with four fingers.

Emelina nods and she looks at Abe, who nods without hesitation.

A centenarian, a burned-out stock trader turned yoga instructor, a home-schooling mom, and a former kindergarten teacher will continue working two murders from a long time ago. If I had any doubts about our success before I looked into her eyes, I do not now. Emelina's diminutive figure is no indication of her outsized determination not to rest until she finds out what happened. I stare at the photo of the young happy couple staring out of the back window of the car with the *Just Married* sign and tin cans hanging from the bumper. We are doing this for Emelina, and we are doing this for them.

CHAPTER EIGHTEEN

"Here is the spider chart for Antoinette and here is the chart for Andrew," Erin says. She displays one on each of her oversized monitors. "Abe and I had to make the connections manually. For instance, who were the people who went to school with them? We used the school yearbooks to identify classmates. Were they on any teams or join any clubs in school? For example, Antoinette was in the drama club. We listed every high schooler that was in the club when she was." All the lines disappear, except for the persons on the drama club purple spider web. "Then we took all those persons and determined if they were still alive." She sorts by dead or alive, and fewer names are connected. "Next, we ran them through my social aggregator programs, and finally Newspaper Archives. Each living person who might have known her through the drama club has a dossier color coded in purple."

Erin clicks through each drama club dossier in alphabetical order. She stops on one person in particular. "Here's Joan Kane. She is seventy-nine years old, graduated the same year as Antoinette, so she has purple, blue, and red lines designating she was a classmate from the same graduating class. Looking at the archives, we see that she was in Antoinette's bridal party." A grainy newspaper captioned notice of Andrew and Antoinette's wedding announcement pops up on the screen.

Abe says, "I took each member of the wedding party designated as a blue line that appears in both Andrew and Antoinette's spider charts and did the same as Erin with the social aggregator programs and the archives program. Erin, please show them names common to both Andrew and Antoinette." She does. He points to the new spider chart. "This yellow line is identical for both of them, but you can see other people from other colored lines that were in both of their worlds."

Erin says, "We only had to do the input once, then the CaseSoft program created the lines and filled in half the dossiers. Joan Kane is still alive, living in the senior center here in town. There are four other people there that knew either Andrew or Antoinette." Erin sorts by street address and the others appear.

I'm impressed. What seemed an impossible task is broken down into manageable steps. "What is this line?" I ask.

Erin says, "These are people that lived near the Bidwells on West Main Street when they were first married and then the people that lived next to them on Elm Street."

"Why does this man have an asterisk next to his name?" I ask.

Abe and Erin share a look. Erin clicks on his dossier and takes a deep breath. "The good news is that he is dead. Johnny Murphy. He died in prison forty-one years ago. He was a sexual predator who victimized women from here to Florida before he got caught."

"I knew his family," Emelina says. "They were devastated."

"By what he had done or by his death?" I ask.

"After the news came out about him, they had to move out of town. People unfairly blamed them for raising a monster," she answered.

"Could he have killed them?" I ask.

Erin shakes her head. "Possibly, but I doubt it. How could he have gotten access to the Devlin mansion to put Andrew in the coal furnace and then drag the steamer trunk in later?"

"Maybe the cops who worked here at the time will know more," I say.

"Johnny Murphy. I never made the connection to him," Emelina says. "But he did live next door."

"How old was he when he lived there?" I ask.

"If he didn't show up in the crisscross directory in 1969, he never would have popped up. He was living with his parents after he got back from an Army hitch in Germany. He was around twenty years old."

"Seems like we have to ask about him," I say. "And what he did he do for work?"

"This is amazing," Emelina interrupts. "I can tell you a little about each one of these people."

"We were hoping you would say that," Abe says.

"How many people are we talking about from all the charts?" I ask.

Abe looks at Erin and she nods her head. "Sixty-eight, give or take," he says.

"Give or take?" I look at them, puzzled by the answer.

"Dementia, Alzheimer's, or too ill from another illness like cancer, which may affect their memory recall," Erin replies. "And there are another twenty-nine persons who later became prominent in town affairs from that time, such as cops, fireman, teachers, and businesspeople, who are still alive."

"Those people are good for background. We suggest you talk to them first so you are better prepared to talk to the people who had closer connections to the couple," Abe says.

"For the out of towners, Emelina could introduce herself and tell them why she is calling. Most of the people will know her or know of her, then she can hand them off to us," Erin adds.

Abe says, "The number of people out of town either

connected to them or having some prominence is roughly half the total. From my days doing cold call selling, it is better to reach out after five p.m. up to about eight forty-five p.m."

"Since the locals are mostly retired, Emelina and Mom can visit them during the day," Erin says just as the oven timer rings. It is five o'clock, and she wants to get dinner on the table in thirty minutes for her family.

"Let's start the calls tonight and start making visits tomorrow," Emelina says.

The memorial service is fresh in our minds, and my mentor doesn't want to waste a minute. We all look at her.

"I've waited for fifty years for answers of what happened to them. After we talk with all these people, we will know much more than we do now," she says.

"What about the police?" Abe asks.

I look at Erin. I know that Abe has a valid question. I also know that what Erin and Abe have done is not crude, cold case investigation. Looking at the dossiers and spider charts, they have given us a competitive advantage, and it's a nice feeling being ahead of the cops for a change and not walking in their footprints. "When we are finished," I say, "we can give them all our hard work. Detective Shafer will grumble, but he will appreciate following behind our snowplow and not having to crash through the snowdrifts by himself." We all look to Erin.

"I hope you all like chicken parm and salad. I made enough for an army," Erin says, anticipating our response.

"I made brownies for dessert," Emelina adds. "I left some in the car."

"I'll call Ken. He and Billy will have to fend for themselves this evening," I say.

"I am sure there are more. Plenty more."

Retired Sheriff's Detective Burt Hodge of Tallahassee, Florida remembers Murphy as if it was yesterday. We wait until almost our quitting time to call him. The excitement of getting started keeps growing, as many people remember Emelina and are happy to talk to her. Learning about their connections to her niece and nephew is interesting. She hands the person off to one of us and then she moves on to the next person. Erin is right. Some people are sharp as a tack and others, not so much. The locator databases are not always accurate, and we have to offer condolences to some surviving family members. Almost all accept the calls or quickly return the calls when they realize we aren't telemarketers. Using three phones, we get return calls while we type notes on as many laptops. Emelina scans the dossiers, adds what she knows about the person, and then we dial and put her on the phone when the connection is made. After some rapport building, she hands our phones back to us and the interviewing begins in earnest.

I am mid-interview with Detective Hodge when he interrupts me. "Call me Burt. I was a cop so long ago, I carried a six-shooter. Back then, rape kits were a new thing. Hospitals in the rural areas were not set up for sexual assault counseling. Over the years and even now with advances in evidence collection, some departments have a backlog of untested kits going back years. Fortunately, Murphy's *modus operandi* was standard. He would drive around until he found his victim and would stake them out and break in while they were sleeping. Women living alone or with roommates who would not be home at night."

"How did he support himself on his way down South?" I have him on speakerphone with an audience on my end.

"He was a booster. He would shoplift high end watches and jewelry in one town and then pawn them in the next. He liked small college towns where a stranger would not be noticed. He hung around hospitals too. Liked nurses."

"Any assaults on the street?" Erin whispers to me. I repeat it to Burt.

"Not that I know of. You gotta understand that it was a very underreported crime back then. Lots of unnecessary shame. More victims come forward these days, but still not what it should be."

"But he got worse, didn't he?" I ask.

"Rape is a crime of violence. The more he got away with it, the bolder he got and the more violent he became."

I dread to ask the question for which I have a partial answer to. "How did he kill them?"

"The sick bastard strangled them."

I watch Emelina turn white.

"How did he get caught?"

"A potential victim heard him come in and when he opened her bedroom door, she was waiting with a softball bat. She played varsity softball. Nearly beat him to death."

"I see. Did he confess to other assaults?"

"No. We had him for several, and the other states were lining up to give him the death penalty when his cellmate at County did us all a favor and punched his ticket."

We talk some more, then I thank him before hanging up. Erin's home office is dead silent. We all wonder what Murphy might have done to his next-door neighbor in Milford when he got back from the Army and whether Andrew became suspicious of him. And if he killed Andrew as well.

CHAPTER NINETEEN

"You weren't a police officer for very long," I say.

It's a dry cold Saturday morning. Emelina and I are sitting on Timothy Sweet's living room couch. His raised ranch is in the newer section of Milford. A farmer's family sold off a large parcel in the 1980s and a big city developer carved it up into a hundred or so quarter-acre plots.

"I could make more money with my side-job than working as a cop," Sweet says. "The hours were better, and I got to still be outside."

His answer seems rehearsed. There is more to his story. Sweet is referring to his landscaping and tree removal business. His kids have taken over the business now, and he splits time between here and a home in Florida. We are lucky we caught him up North.

"What was it like being a policeman back in the late Sixties?"

"It was busier than nowadays with the protests and all. Milford wasn't growing. A lot of the good jobs moved out of town. We ran three shifts, had a detective, a juvenile officer, and a jailer."

"Who else worked with you back then?" I know some of the names and can test his memory.

"There was the chief, Herman Kenrick, and three sergeants, Bill O'Hara, Sam Roman, Hubie Carroll. The detective was Jack Dougherty, and the juvie officer was Sandra Egan."

I nod as he rattles off nine patrolmen. "That's some memory."

"I've lived in town my whole life and would see them all the time. I even hired some of them to work for me part-time. Kenrick's brother did plumbing and heating and hired some of the guys too. I was the youngest guy on the force. The tax base was shrinking. Some of the guys were Vietnam vets, so they had preference for any promotions. I was gonna get stuck working midnights, weekends, and holidays for a long time."

"Okay." There is more, so I let him roll.

"So, over the years when a guy would quit, they wouldn't replace him. When Kenrick retired, the senior sergeant served as acting chief, and it went that way until all the sergeants retired or quit. Now what do you have? Two full-timers and two part-timers with State Police coverage overnight? Won't be long before it is just the Stateys responding to all the calls."

I sense he wants to say more, so I ask, "What else about back then?"

He looks over at Emelina. "You knew what it was like back then, Ms. Bidwell. There were two sets of rules. One for the big-shots and one for the little people. I got into it a few times with Kenrick. I talked to him man-to-man outside of Borough Hall once at three in the morning after I arrested one of Milford's finer citizens for beating his wife. I asked the chief none too politely to give me a list of who I could arrest and who I couldn't. He didn't like that. I told him it would make my job much easier. The straw that broke the camel's back is when he un-arrested a peeping Tom I caught outside of a no-tell motel."

"Why did he do that?" Emelina asked.

"The guy was a Catholic priest. He was wearing his clerical collar under a windbreaker and no, he didn't have permission to be looking in the ground floor window of the couple going at it. The Archbishop got the chief out of bed. Kenrick came down to Borough Hall with a coat over his pajamas before the pervert's fingerprints were even dry. I've never seen him that angry. I thought he was gonna bust a blood vessel or something."

We sit quietly as he stews over events from a very long time ago.

"Kenrick wasn't as squeaky clean as he acted," Sweet continues. "He had his hand in a lot of things. He must have had something on the mayor. Do you wonder why he was the last Chief of Police in this town?"

Emelina interrupts his train of thought with, "Do you remember taking the missing person report of my niece, Antoinette Bidwell?

"A missing person's report?"

"It was Christmas Eve, 1969."

He screws his face up in thought. "I'm sorry, Ma'am." Sweet shakes his head. "I quit the force a few months later. Spring season is always big for landscaping, and I decided I had enough of Kenrick, so I took the leap."

"Tell us about Johnny Murphy," I say.

"Who?"

"He lived next to Emelina's niece and nephew that year on Elm Street," I say.

"I went to school with his older sister, Megan, if it's the same Murphy family. Didn't he get in trouble somewhere down South?"

We nod to him. "Rape and murder."

"That's right, I remember now."

"He came home after serving in the Army in Germany. Do you know what he did after he was discharged?" I ask.

"Not a clue," Sweet says.

We ask him about which cops are still around and who have

gone to the big roll call in the sky. He tells us that policing is not good for one's health and none of the roster from back then are still alive.

"It took me a long time to get it out of my system," he says. "When I see the cruisers flying by with the lights and sirens on, I miss it. I wake up from dreams of being in uniform, only problem is I am not wearing any pants. In those dreams it is kinda difficult to stand up at roll call."

We all laugh and get up at the same time. He walks us to the door and promises to tell us if he remembers anything that can help us find out what happened to Andrew and Antoinette.

We get outside and remember how cold it is as we cinch up our scarves and pull our hand-knit wool hats down over our ears. Emelina's Mercury doesn't warm up on our drive to the Senior Center.

We save Joan Kane for last. The others recall who from their graduating class went to the fiftieth high school reunion, but everyone just assumed that Antoinette went to Broadway or Hollywood. A couple of the retirees had been to the funeral service and were shocked to hear how she died.

Joan was not Antoinette's maid of honor but was one of her closest friends, we find out.

"I was devastated when I never heard from her," Joan says. "I was angry at her for years thinking that she disappeared without saying goodbye."

"Did you ever think something bad happened to her?" I ask.

"No, I thought she deserted Andrew and was too ashamed to tell anybody about it."

"Why did you think that?"

"When she didn't give him children, he became cold and aloof. I don't think it was her fault that they didn't have kids, but all the same he blamed it on her."

I can see Emelina getting uncomfortable with that opinion, but she is wise enough to know that family are sometimes the last people to find something out.

"Before she left, I mean disappeared, she told me that Andrew had become withdrawn, and she couldn't reach him. She asked me for advice. I told her that they should get counseling. Neither of them had health insurance and it would have to come out of their pocket."

"Do you know where they worked?" I ask.

"Andrew was a quality assurance manager at Milford Specialty Steel—they are out of business now—and she worked as a bookkeeper at Milford Coal & Ice." Joan giggles with a distant memory.

"What?"

"I remember before everybody got refrigerators, they would come around and deliver ice blocks in the spring and summer and then coal in the fall and winter. They are out of business too."

"They used horse drawn carriages through the Depression and kept using the horses during World War II because of the gas rationing," Emelina says.

"That's right." Joan smiles at the memory. "I was really young, but I remember the Milford Coal & Ice carriage being pulled by two black horses."

I make a mental note about them delivering coal. There may be something at the library about them. Photocopies of old photos may help jog people's memories. We have Antoinette and Andrew's high school photos as well.

I change the subject. "Joan, you know Antoinette never left Milford. She was strangled and stuffed in a steamer trunk hidden behind a fake wall. Can you think of anybody who could have done something like that?

"No, that's the thing. The last couple of times I talked to her before Christmas, she seemed really happy. She was looking forward to the holidays. Whatever was bad between Andrew and her seemed to be fixed, but she didn't tell me what it was. I just assumed they patched things up." Joan pauses and thinks carefully about what she says next. "But after she disappeared, I thought her happiness came from finally making a decision to leave Andrew and to leave Milford."

"I guess you were wrong," Emelina says sternly.

Before I let that sink in, I try to rescue the interview. "Did you know Johnny Murphy?"

"There was talk about him getting in serious trouble down South."

"Did you know he was Antoinette's neighbor?"

My question stuns Joan. Her eyes get big behind her glasses. "Oh dear." She looks away from both of us and stands up from her rocker. Emelina and I watch her pace between the TV stand and the living room window facing the oval driveway and parking area in front of the center.

Her distress is palpable. I am wondering if she was a victim of an unreported attack. Did I just open an old wound?

She sits back down and her hands tremble as she lifts her teacup of tepid milky liquid to her lips. I can see her debating if she is going to say anything. She sets the tea down and looks at Emelina. "Antoinette said her neighbor was having a hard time finding a job after he came back from the service, and she got him a job at Milford Coal & Ice as a delivery man. She never said his name, but now I realize who she was talking about."

CHAPTER TWENTY

"Johnny Murphy worked at Milford Coal & Ice the same time as Antoinette," I repeat to Erin from Emelina's Mercury. My teeth are chattering from the cold, but I am excited for finding this lead. It's too soon to say we broke the case, but it's a piece of information I am not going to sit on with Shafer.

"You said he was a delivery man. It was wintertime when Antoinette disappeared. He would know who was getting coal deliveries." She is quick on the uptake.

"And he would know who stopped getting coal delivered in the spring when Andrew disappeared," I add.

"But that still doesn't explain the partition," Erin tells us on speakerphone.

"I agree. It is too soon to say there is a solid connection here, but we can't ignore it either."

"I'll dig up everything I can on Milford Coal & Ice and keep you posted." Erin disconnects the call.

Emelina and I aren't ready to accept that Murphy was the killer, but the coincidences are too hard to ignore. Until yesterday, we didn't have any connections, and finding a sexual offender as the next-door neighbor is pretty compelling.

I had printed out the dossiers and put them in order by address to make a big circle, so we don't waste time driving back and forth around the county. Ken helped me last night by shuffling them in this order. He knows this neck of the woods like the back of his hand. We are in the driveway of Antoinette's maid of honor, Gloria Michaels Kennedy.

"She was like that," Emelina says before we review Gloria's write-up.

"Who?"

"My niece. She was always helping people. Whether it was a coat drive or making Thanksgiving dinners for poor folks, she would always pitch in and volunteer. Hard to think that that was how Murphy repaid her."

I can't think of an appropriate response. Erin could go on for hours from her encyclopedic knowledge of true crime how the cops learned that it was the neighbor after arresting the spouse, only to have forensics clear them. Once they stumbled onto the neighbor, the pieces of the puzzle fell into place. Time after time, the detectives had tunnel vision and tried to make the evidence fit their theory as opposed to have the evidence lead them to the correct suspect who was hiding in plain sight. This was the gospel according to Erin LeGrande.

I say, "Please let me do the talking after you introduce us, Em. I am not as emotionally attached to what these people tell us as you are, and we don't want to shut down their recollections if we don't like what they are saying, okay?" I try to gently remind my mentor that we have different roles here, especially after the last couple of interviews.

I add, after I knock on Gloria's front door, "At the end of the interview, I will turn to you and ask you if there is anything you want to clear up, okay?"

"You're right. I am hearing things about my niece and my nephew that don't match my memory."

Gloria opens the door and Emelina tells her, "Hi Gloria, do you remember me? I am Antoinette Sorrento's aunt. She married my nephew, Andrew."

"Yes, please come in. I saw you at the memorial service yesterday. It was very nice of you to do that for them. I am sorry for your loss, Ms. Bidwell."

"Call me Emelina. This is Gwendolyn Strong. You may know her from town. She replaced me at Milford Elementary as the kindergarten teacher. She is helping me to try to figure out what happened all those years ago."

"Call me Gwen," I say.

"Nice to meet you, Gwen. I am not sure what I can tell you. It's been a long time. Please come in. It's too cold out there."

She leads us to her kitchen and past the living room, where her husband is sleeping in his recliner with the TV turned on loud. The smell of tomato sauce reminds me that we skipped lunch. The timer rings and Gloria removes two dozen meatballs from the oven and drops them one by one into the crockpot. When she's done, she says, "Okay, what would you like to know?"

Emelina and I take seats at the kitchen table while Gloria remains standing by the oven.

"You were her maid of honor for her wedding to Andrew," I say.

Short and heavyset with gray hair cut short, wearing an apron over a simple pastel colored dress and sensible shoes, Gloria appears to be exactly halfway between my age and that of my mentor. She is taken aback by my statement and stammers, "Yes, how did you know that?"

I make a show of retrieving a photocopy of the marriage announcement from the afternoon paper and hand it to her.

She reads it and hands it back. "That's right."

I am reminded by her opening response to our inquiry that she is not sure what she can tell us. Does that mean she has to be careful with her words? She was Antoinette's maid of honor, and she came to the memorial service yesterday. Certainly, she must know something about the bride and the groom.

"I remember it was a nice wedding and we all had a good time," she says, turning to busy herself with a stubborn pot to wash.

We watch Gloria spend an inordinate amount of time scrubbing the pot. Emelina and I look at each other and we decide to wait her out. When that pot is washed, she dries it and then reaches for the baking tray where the meatballs left their marks.

Before she can turn her back to us again, I say, "Gloria, please tell us about how you knew Antoinette."

"We were best friends in high school and were in the band together. When Andrew proposed, she asked me to be her maid of honor."

"And afterwards?"

"Pretty soon, I married Dan and started a family." She tackles the baking tray next and goes through the same routine of turning her back to us while washing and drying. Before I can ask another question, she reaches for the mixing bowl where she had added the breading and spices to the ground beef.

What is she not telling us? By not talking to us, she is not lying to us. I shrug with palms up at Emelina and decide to try a different approach.

I broach this new approach with, "We were told that just before Christmas of 1969 that Antoinette was pretty happy. Tell us what know about that."

She stays turned away from us and replies, "That's a long time ago. Must be over fifty years."

"Thank you for your response, Gloria, but could you please answer my question?" The words are not so gentle this time.

She turns slowly and finishes wiping her dry hands drier. She fiddles with the strings to her apron and avoids eye contact. "I'm not sure what good it will do after all these years."

I take a gamble. "We just came from Joan Kane's house, and she told us you would know why Antoinette was happy even though her marriage with Andrew was not what it once had been."

Emelina leans in and says gently, "No time for secrets, Gloria. We need to know."

Gloria looks at Emelina and then to me. I nod my head. "Fifty years is a long time to keep a secret. You can let it go."

She turns back to the sink, sees that it is empty, then reaches for a ladle and stirs the meatballs absent-mindedly. She sets the ladle down on counter and moves to what would be her normal seat at the table. She stares at her hands and pinches her eyes closed, but that can't stop the tears from leaking out. She shudders and tries to choke back a sob. The sobs become crying, and she holds her hands over her eyes. I sit there staring at her, not knowing whether to comfort her or to allow her release what was bottled up inside.

Emelina reaches her hands out and takes both of Gloria's hands into hers. "I know what she told you. It's okay." Turning to me, Emelina says, "Remember when you asked me if Antoinette could have killed herself and I told you she would never do that? I didn't tell you why I knew that." Looking back at Antoinette's maid of honor, she says, "It's okay, Gloria, go ahead and tell us why your best friend couldn't kill herself."

Gloria straightens up and uses the bottom of the apron on her eyes, then takes a deep inhale. "She was pregnant. It proved that it was not her fault why she and Andrew couldn't have kids. I thought she had run away with the baby's father and started a new life, a happier life, then they discovered her bones here in town a couple weeks ago. I didn't know what to think."

CHAPTER TWENTY-ONE

Forget meditating this morning. My mind is whirling like a tornado through Dorothy's Kansas. Even Billy feels my agitation and struggles to find a comfortable position inside my crossed legs. The only centering thought I have is a question, one I am shooting like a silent invisible dart across the circle at Emelina: Gosh, Emelina Bidwell, do you think it would have been important to know your niece was pregnant when she went missing?

Abe picks up on my vibe and again repeats the guided meditation of feeling our breath in our nostrils and then in our throats, followed by the rising and falling in our chests, and lastly the in and out of our abdomens. He goes through the body scan one more time to fill up the hour. I will let her tell Abe what I already told Erin the night before. The minute she dropped me off on my doorstep, I walked Billy around the house a dozen times before Erin calmed me down. Emelina and I had talked about what more Gloria had said after she dropped the bombshell on me. I knew it was best for me to wait a day before confronting my longest friend and mentor about why she didn't tell us about Antoinette's pregnancy.

If there is a competition for doing moon salutations mechanically, I would win first-prize today. I turn my mat in a way to avoid eye contact with her. During the final resting pose, I finally get over my own stubbornness and ask myself why Emelina needed to withhold Antoinette's situation from me and Detective Shafer, knowing that it might be the key to the murders.

Emelina never married and never had children. She never hinted to me why that was the case. She was fashionably past dating age when I first met her. This was before I met Ken. I told her about some of the boys I dated, before deeming my man as "the one." She was there for me when I got pregnant with both Erin and Wesley, and she celebrated all three of my grandchildren. I find it hard to believe that she could not think that her niece's pregnancy would not be germane to her disappearance. Was it because her nephew was not the father and having a baby out of wedlock was sinful? Religion can make for some strange reasoning. I don't know Emelina to be outwardly religious. She does not attend a church in town and professes no spiritual leanings. Focusing on her now, I can sense a deeper reason for her reticence, and with that I began to feel some compassion for her. Does she harbor guilt for not taking any actions when they both disappeared? Is there something she is not forgiving herself for that didn't allow her to tell us what she knew back in the day? I have to remind myself that my friend is dealing with the discovery of the remains of her closest family relations fifty years later and finding out they were both murdered. Is she walking a tightrope of not telling us everything and hoping that we can solve it without her own secrets being exposed?

Erin reminded me last night that if Emelina was private investigator Bill Spencer's client, he would have to respect his client's wishes to go about his investigation without all the facts and that it might jeopardize the outcome of the case.

If it came to that, would I have the heart to tell her that we can't go on any further without knowing what else she is withholding? If she decides she wants to tell me or Shafer, that's fine, but who am I to chide this woman while she is mourning the loss of her nearest relatives?

I help Abe and Em put back the yoga mats, bolsters, and blankets. We have another full day of interviewing. I tell Emelina that I am walking Billy home and she can meet me there. I need some more time to get over my perceived slight. How could we know each other all these years and she not feel like she could share a gamechanger with me?

As Billy smells every tree, fire hydrant, and signpost on the way home, I realize it has been pretty much a one-way street. I was growing into Emelina's shoes as Milford Elementary's kindergarten teacher. She watched me grow from a confidence-lacking college student into a teacher, wife, mother, and grandmother. What did I know about her? How did she change or grow over the decades? She is a private person, not one to gossip or engage in frivolous chatter. A model of self-sufficiency, it was only recently that she decided to share her recipes with me. Maybe turning 100 years old gives her the feeling that she needs to consider leaving a legacy through me.

The disappearance of Andrew and Antoinette was unfinished business in her life, but she didn't expect them to be murdered and hidden away. Can I respect her privacy and swallow hard on the fact that there are things I might never know about her or this case?

I hear hammering upstairs when I bring Billy in through my home's back door. Ken's working on our place today. He will have Billy as his buddy.

Emelina pulls up into my driveway and I get in. The car is warmed up nicely. I reach down into the milk crate we are using as a poor man's filing cabinet and tell her who's next on the list and their home address. She will refresh herself on their dossier in their driveway before we knock on their door. Maybe she knows that I will eventually get to the truth of what happened and that this investigation will not be an act of futility.

As we bump along the snow rutted roads, I recall Emelina had this maddening way of letting a young student teacher learn things for myself when it was well within her power to show me. The mistakes I made allowed me to appreciate how I got from stumbling in the dark to seeing the light. She knew the answers but made me search for them. It served me well when I raised my own kids. Both kids have thanked me more than once for allowing them to learn how to do things rather than me taking control and making it easy for them. Reframing the bombshell revelation from yesterday this way makes it easy to understand why I must solve this case without her giving me all the clues.

We stop the car in Andrew's best man's driveway. Joe Bonner was his best friend, and he and his wife went out often with Andrew and Antoinette. His wife Rose died a year ago, Emelina tells me as she peruses the dossier. It will be interesting to hear what Andrew may have shared with his best friend before and after Antoinette went missing. I wonder if anyone had talked to him about Andrew when Andrew went missing.

We knock on the door and are greeted by a sandy-haired woman about my age who tells us that she is Joe's daughter. Emelina explains to her the reason for our visit.

Joe's daughter shakes her head. "It all happened real fast. One day he was doing great, but he took a fall around before Thanksgiving and broke his hip. The trip to the hospital and rehab accelerated his slide." We walk in and see him leaning uncomfortably against the side of his wheelchair. He is positioned in front of the television. A cruel saying forms in my head and I realize there must be a better way of saying that the lights are on, but nobody's home. He looks at us and I realize that he wouldn't know Andrew Bidwell from the mailman. We thank her for her time and shut the front door behind us. I hear another door shut on our investigation.

The car engine rumbles to life as I make brief handwritten notes of the visit. Emelina peruses the next dossier. This was our routine the day before, as I would finish the notes of each interview and then act as her navigator.

She waits until we are stopped at the town's main traffic signal and says, "When Antoinette told me she was pregnant, she swore me to secrecy. She hadn't told Andrew. What does that tell you? Abortions were not legal yet, but she was determined to have the baby, that much I know. I promised her I would do whatever I could to help her. Then she disappeared. I thought that she would have the baby and give it up to adoption and return to Milford. But as the months went by, I assumed she ran off with the baby's father. Poor Andrew, he never caught on. He was twisted with grief. He couldn't work and began drinking too much. He thought something bad happened to her. It turns out he was right. He was supposed to meet Chief Kenrick and tell him his suspicions. He didn't come home that night or the next or the next. Pretty soon, it was clear that Andrew disappeared too without telling a soul where he was going. For years, I daydreamed that he went searching for her and that someday Andrew, Antoinette, and the baby would return and everything would be normal again."

"Then you learn what happened to her from me. Before we could make any sense of it, Ken finds what happened to Andrew," I say.

"I learned they both were killed and hidden away around the same time," she says.

"Did Andrew suspect someone kidnapped Antoinette?"

"Not exactly." She stares at the green signal as the car behind us toots twice. She drives slowly into the quickie-mart parking lot. She anticipates my next question. "He suspected she may have had a boyfriend."

"And he told you."

"Yes. He swore me to secrecy, and he told me he was going to inform Chief Kenrick." Looking over at me, she asks, "Can you understand why I didn't tell you about their secrets, Gwendolyn? For years, I expected one or both to show up again."

"You have always been a private person." I have a harder time with what I say next. "I will respect your wishes."

"I am giving you all my secret recipes, dear. But in this situation, I was sworn to secrecy. I have been carrying that burden for over fifty years." She puts the car in park. "The only thing you take to your grave is your reputation, Gwendolyn. I promised my niece and nephew that I would keep their secrets. Promises are promises."

"But why did you keep these secrets after you learned they were murdered? Didn't you see that telling would help us find their killers?" I try to keep the irritation out of my voice. I fail.

"It doesn't matter if they were dead or alive. Promises are promises. If you want to stop now, I can take you home."

I can't argue with that logic. Being pregnant with another man's child would have brought shame onto Antoinette back then. Her remaining cousins could care less now. It must have to do with leaving one's legacy and how you want people to remember you. Or in this this case, how Emelina wants people to remember her niece.

She is giving me a plausible reason to quit. She is not forthcoming with relevant information. I have to trust my mentor and friend of many years that her wisdom passes my understanding. I wrestle with my decision. It is not an easy one. I can quit, or I can play by her one rule. Finally, I decide that I'm more curious to see where this goes than to be upset that she is withholding pertinent information from me.

"You're making me work for it, Emelina, just like when I was a student teacher. Who are we visiting next?"

CHAPTER TWENTY-TWO

"I questioned Mardell's kids about the time period when the partition was built," Shafer says. "They were not forthcoming with me right away. They freaked out when I told them what was found behind the basement partition. I got their attention real fast when I told them both victims were murdered. They told me it was built while they lived there. After the partition went up, they were not allowed to play in the basement. Their father said that there were rats in the basement."

Ken hadn't said anything about rodent infestation. I deduce their father didn't want them exploring down there for other reasons.

The conference room in the Borough Hall is a fishbowl. Word will be out in minutes that the State Police are meeting with Gwen Strong and Emelina Bidwell. They have their reasons to make it obvious they are talking with us. If the Mayor wants to complain to Shafer's commander again, he will know that it is falling on deaf ears. Local interference in two killings under the State's jurisdiction will not be tolerated any longer.

Barney also contributes to the meeting. As long as the State Police are calling the shots, he is safe from political fallout.

"Their father sold the property in the late 1980's and they moved up to Carolyn Heights," he says.

We act appreciative but we already have copies of the deed transfer in our files. Carolyn Heights was a parcel of land, sold off by the Bloodstone Family Trust, with views of Milford and the river beyond. A dozen McMansions on hillside lots overlooking the river were developed and gobbled up quickly.

Emelina and I are sitting across from Shafer and Barney. After our little fork in the road moment, we had made quick work of the remaining persons in town who knew the Bidwell couple. Memories dulled by the passing years or persons with only a limited knowledge didn't add any more pieces to the puzzle.

Barney watches as Shafer gives me copies of the index cards I already know about. I take the copies from him with all the respect due him for acting against the interest of the Mayor, for whom he is not beholden the way Barney is. I tell him that I have a newspaper photo from back in the day of Timothy Sweet and Chief Kenrick, then give him a copy of my notes from my interview.

"What is this about a Johnny Murphy you were asking Sweet about?" Shafer asks.

I produce a copy of the work that Erin had done. "Murphy was awaiting trial for murders and sexual assaults in Tallahassee, Florida."

"So?" Barney asks.

"Here is a copy of the Cole Directory from 1969 showing a Johnny Murphy returning from Army service and living in the residence next to Andrew and Antoinette."

Shafer takes it with real interest and scans it closely. "I'll be damned."

I hand him my interview of Joan Kane, a member of Antoinette's bridal party who told us that Antoinette worked at Milford Coal & Ice and helped her neighbor get a job there. He reads it slowly and goes back over the crisscross directory copy, then back to the interview with Burt Hodge, and finally the newspaper clipping about Murphy's arrest. As he finishes with one piece of information, he hands it to Barney. He pushes the newspaper articles about Murphy getting killed in prison into Barney's eager hands and looks at me. I've pulled the rabbit out of the hat for him, and he's trying to figure out how I did it.

"I had help from my daughter and Abe Schatz," I say. "We created a dossier for everybody who had some connection to the couple. That's the short answer."

"This is top-notch stuff, Mrs. Strong."

"Thank you, Detective Shafer." I am blushing and don't try to hide it. I will take a well-earned compliment from a professional homicide investigator when it is offered. "There are issues about the timing of the placement of the bodies in the basement and when the partition was built."

"Can we assume the partition was built shortly after the permit was taken out for the oil burner?" he asks.

"Yes. The permit was taken out in the homeowner's name and not the contractor's company," I say.

Emelina asks, "Could Murphy have had something to do with building the partition?"

Barney looks up from the last newspaper article and says, "That would make sense. He could bring both bodies down to the basement and then wall that section off."

"Ken said, and I think you will agree, that it would still take two people to bring the bodies down to the basement."

Barney nods.

"Two killers?" Emelina asks.

"That, or one killer with an accomplice," Shafer says.

"After the fact?" I ask.

"Yes," he says.

"You have to know somebody very well to ask them to drag a body in a carpet through a house and into the basement," I say.

"Not necessarily." He shows me a photo of the coal chute opening that had been bricked over and was now uncovered. "The circumference of the carpet would fit down the coal chute. It could have been dropped down from outside." He shows me the two measurements.

"Just like a load of coal," I say.

"That is why this Murphy character is really important," Shafer says.

"He would know when they stopped delivering coal, but could still get access to the coal furnace," Barney says.

I can't believe I am spit-balling with the police on how Murphy could do this. "The steamer trunk could have been brought in when they installed the oil burner. Nobody would notice or care it about it coming in the house, but it would still take two people," I say.

"One could be unsuspecting," Barney says. "I wish I had a nickel for every time I've helped somebody clean stuff out of their parents' house."

"So, one person who knew what was in the trunk could have done it with an unsuspecting accomplice," Shafer says.

My findings about Murphy earns me a chair at the big people's table. "But making a coal delivery is different from building a partition."

"And knowing when the partition would be built and getting the steamer trunk behind it beforehand requires some more finesse than a laborer could pull off," Shafer says.

I can see his balloon deflating somewhat.

Barney is still hot to trot on Murphy and pinning a double homicide on a sexual predator with access to both victims. The knowledge of when the coal furnace would no longer be used could close the case without necessarily solving it, a result that

Erin and I had personal knowledge of from our first foray into true crime.

"There's something else. Forensics found hair samples in the steamer trunk that were not human," Shafer says. He turns a sheet of paper around and points to the lab analysis findings at the bottom.

"Horsehair?"

"Yes. Combined with the fact that the trunk was handcrafted in Saratoga, New York, it might have something to do with horse racing," Shafer explains.

Barney adds, "Saratoga has a summer racing season. It's a hangout for rich people."

"The kind of crowd Mardell was part of," Emelina says.

We haven't even scratched the surface of the homeowner's background, and here Barney and Emelina are, filling in some blanks.

My thoughts go to Carly Simon's song "You're So Vain." I run the lyrics through my head quickly. Can we add Mick Jagger to the list of suspects? "The trunk was built before automobiles. Could the horsehair have come from the trunk being transported on horse-drawn carriages?" I ask.

Shafer replies, "I am assuming that the trunk transported gear for horses as the hair was embedded in the inside only."

Since we are all buddy-buddy today, thanks to my Johnny Murphy lead, I take a chance with another question. "Any luck with the drapes?"

"High-end and imported from Italy. We weren't able to pull any fingerprints," Shafer says.

Barney conjectures, "Imported Italian drapes, Saratoga racing, being able to hide two bodies in a historical landmark. Doesn't sound like a coal delivery guy could pull that off." He's not so sure about Murphy now.

"But you just said that you helped friends move stuff out of parent's basements. Expensive drapes in an old steamer trunk could have been in the basement already," I say.

"The newspaper clippings?" Emelina asks.

"Added to fill the trunk up so the body would not make noise as it was being moved," Shafer says. "But we still can't rule out that the trunk could have been in the basement already."

"Johnny Murphy. T.J. Mardell. Johnny Murphy. T.J. Mardell. What about Johnny Murphy and T.J. Mardell?" I ask.

We all put on our thinking caps for that one.

"Working as a team for what reason?" Shafer asks.

"A sexual predator and a car dealer?" Emelina asks.

"A sexual predator and a car dealer who is also a sexual predator?" Shafer adds an interesting twist.

"They do their thing with Mrs. Bidwell and knock off Mr. Bidwell to cover their tracks?" Barney's statement is formed as a question.

"But why hide the evidence in your basement?" I ask, then throw some water on their thinking. "Mardell would have some serious explaining to do if someone got back behind the partition and made the discoveries."

"Mardell has the work done, and Murphy knows he can somehow get the bodies back there and sealed off with no one being the wiser," Shafer says.

"Did Milford Coal & Ice do oil delivery?" Barney asks.

"I can check." They look at me. I add, "Residential coal and oil delivery was advertised in the newspapers. It wouldn't take long to scan the microfilm at the library for their advertisements."

Emelina shakes her head. "I doubt they did both. Oil replaced coal the way gas replaces oil."

"And hydro, solar, and wind will replace both of them eventually," I say. "At least we will find out who did oil deliveries and installed oil burners."

So far, we haven't crossed swords with Shafer and Williams.

That the police wanted to get the lab testing done first before they did any field work bought us some time. We have one more stop later this afternoon by special appointment, and we are getting close to that time.

I take a chance on asking one more question of Shafer. "How did it go with Truscott Daniels?"

He smiles. "He gives his regards."

"I bet he does."

"Was the photo you told me about on the wall next to the window?"

"Close to his desk," I say.

He nods. "Was it about eight inches tall by eleven inches wide?"

"Yes."

"The empty place on the wall still had the nail protruding from where that photo hung. You must have really hit home when you asked him about it for him to take it off the wall. It probably hung there for a long time. The paint was not faded and stood out like a sore thumb." He laughs.

"I can tell you I recognized Daniels, Meade, and Burgess Bloodstone only because two of them were standing in front of me and I had seen photos of Benjamin's father numerous times when I looked at the newspapers on microfilms at the library."

"I asked him about it," Shafer says, "and he looked at me straight in the eye and asked, 'What photo?' I went over to the wall and traced my finger around the spot and tapped the nail and said, 'That photo.'"

Shafer chuckles, then continues. "Daniels shrugged his shoulders and told me 'I'll have to ask the cleaning company.' He's a lousy liar for a lawyer. When I asked him about his client list from the 1970s, he said it was confidential, even if he could remember."

"How often do you think he's been questioned as a material witness in two murders?" I ask.

"You could count it on one finger. It was fun tweaking him, especially after sending the Mayor as a messenger boy to my boss."

Shafer doesn't tell me what he has planned next and doesn't ask me what I am working on. We run out of steam, and I thank the boys in blue for their time running over the leads with me.

Coming at this investigation from different angles seems to work for us. Shafer turns over a card, then I do. It's not like the killer is poised to strike again. It might turn out that Murphy attacked Antoinette and killed Andrew to cover his tracks. I could live with clearing the case that way, but only after we exhaust all the leads, including finding out who Antoinette's boyfriend was. For a moment I consider the theory that Andrew killed Antoinette when he found out she was pregnant to this other unnamed fellow and killed her in retaliation. I quickly discard that theory because of how and when their bodies were sealed in the Devlin mansion basement. I glance at my friend and mentor and stifle my resentment at her hiding two keys to the case.

Barney, always a gentleman, walks us to the lobby.

I say to him, "Thank you, Barney, for setting up this meeting and sharing the index cards with us."

"We might have learned about Murphy, but you saved us a lot of time and energy, Mrs. Strong," he replies.

We chat some more, but my attention is drawn to the floor-to-ceiling display case outside of the police offices. The history of the Milford Police Department is on display here. Black and white photos from the earliest days, along with the tools of policing, are laid out left to right in chronological order. The uniform styles changed through the years, from frocks and tunics to tailored military-styled uniforms. Beards and long moustaches disappeared over time. Bicycles and horses were replaced by Indian and Harley motorcycles. Plymouths with a single rotating red light on top gave way to Crown Victoria interceptors. Hats and caps changed too. A hundred and fifty years of handcuffs and batons are displayed. Knives, brass knuckles, and drug paraphernalia made for some interesting confiscations. A vintage police radio sits on a table, with photos of the old dispatch room holding a prominent position in the display. Each time period is punctuated by a portrait or photo of the police chief in power at the time.

I stare at Herman Kenrick and wonder if he ever had that meeting with Andrew Bidwell. He is commemorated as the town's last chief with a wooden triangular glass-enclosed case displaying his badge above his gun, and a brass plaque, tarnished from the years on display, notes how he bravely protected and served the fine folks of Milford.

We say our goodbyes and make the short walk on cleared sidewalks to the Historical Society, where Karen Manilla is waiting for us.

"When both the *Times Herald* and *Courier* went out of business, we were able to get their morgue files," Karen says.

"Morgue files?" Emelina asks.

"Both newspapers kept clippings by subjects of interest or persons' names along with all of the photography the papers took. When a reporter wanted to do a background story, they would visit the morgue files. Both papers went out of circulation before the internet, so the photos were filed by month and year and the people or subjects of interest alphabetically."

Erin has learned about morgue files from working with the intelligence analyst she is assigned to with the FBI. She hooked me up with Karen, who is closer in age to Emelina.

"I have three things I want to concentrate on. First, Milford's mansions and their owners," I say.

She writes this down.

I continue, "Second, anything to do with Milford Coal & Ice. And lastly, the photo collection for 1969 and 1970."

I can't take credit for the last one. That was Erin's idea.

"The morgue files are kept in dry storage, and I have to retrieve them," Karen tells me. "We make a run every other week. Our next run is this Friday."

It is the day before President's weekend. Emelina and I will be baking like crazy on Sunday and Monday for the Chamber of Commerce party.

"Can we come back Tuesday?" I ask.

"In the afternoon. Our hours are from noon to eight on Tuesdays. We do that Tuesdays and Thursdays to accommodate the out-of-town genealogists."

We thank Karen, then leave. Walking back to Emelina's car, I ask her, "Are you up for making the last calls to out of towners tonight? I can check with Erin and Abe."

"Did you forget what today is?" she asks.

"It's Wednesday," I say. What is the significance of Wednesday? We've worked this case on the last two previous Wednesdays.

"It's not too late to get him something?"

"Who?" I ask.

She smiles at me mischievously. "Your husband."

Then it hits me. "I forgot it's Valentine's Day!" I shriek.

"Not to worry, I have some brownies in a tin in the trunk. We can stop at Phil's Pharmacy for a card."

Secrets be damned. I can't stay mad at this woman.

"I didn't plan anything special for dinner. I have Sunday's meatloaf and mashed potatoes as leftovers."

"He knows you are working late with me today. Maybe he will surprise you."

My tongue is smarting from a paper cut from trying to lick the envelope for my guy's Valentine Card while riding shotgun with a centenarian whose car tires are magnets for potholes. Billy gives me a kiss when I open the door while juggling the milk crate of dossiers and Emelina's tin of brownies. I am hit by the smell of grilled meats and realize that my man is making dinner. I am ravenous. The lights are turned low, candles are burning. Crosby, Stills, Nash and Young are on Pandora. Our best china is out, and two glasses of red wine sit in front of cutlery over cloth napkins. What did I do to deserve this man?

He carries a platter of sizzling steaks and aluminum-foiled baked potatoes in through the kitchen sliders from the gas grill on the patio.

"Right on time," he says.

I did casually mention to him that I thought I would be home by six and he must have had his listening ears on. To the side of my place setting is a card in a much drier envelope, along with a wrapped box of Milford's finest chocolates. I only get them on special occasions. My thoughts turn away from food for a moment. Those thoughts will have to wait until we are in another room of our house.

"How was your day?" he asks while placing my hot meal on a plate.

"Are you sure you want me to talk about my day?"

"Yes, I am. I bet you did a nice show and tell with Detective Shafer and Officer Williams."

This a complete turnaround from when he didn't want to talk after he made the grisly discoveries. If Erin asked me this question, dinner would fly by without me tasting a morsel. But Ken took the time to make dinner, get me my favorite gift, and give me his undivided attention. "Let's save it for later. I just want to eat and talk about how good we have it."

CHAPTER TWENTY-THREE

Clean-up goes smoothly, and Ken and I decide to finish the wine bottle by the fire. Billy is snuggled between us and is getting a double belly rub. Somebody is in doggie heaven. I know Ken wants to hear how things went today, so I start out slowly. "I almost pulled the plug today. Emelina told me that her nephew suspected that Antoinette had a boyfriend, but that he swore her to secrecy. She wouldn't tell me who the boyfriend was."

"Like Antoinette's secret of being pregnant and the baby most likely not being Andrew's," he replies.

I say, "That's right. I asked her if she was prepared to not find out who killed them if it meant keeping secrets. She basically told me that she made a promise, she was going to honor it, and she could drive me home if I liked."

"Even if the promises were made to murder victims?" he asks.

"Emelina is a very private person. I am not sure why she didn't marry or have children. What do we really know about her? In all the years that I have known her, I never saw a gentleman suitor. She was the former kindergarten teacher, and I was the new one. Besides being a scratch baker with irrepressible energy, what do we know about her? She is there for all of us and never wants to be beholden to another single human being. If you tell her a secret, she will take it to her grave."

"She did give you two clues," Ken says. "Andrew couldn't make babies, and he suspected a boyfriend."

"True. Also that he was going to take that information to Chief Kenrick."

"Who's been dead for how long?"

"1979, a couple of years after he retired and moved to Florida."

"So you can't ask him. How about any detectives working at the time?"

"All dead."

"What's left to do?" he asks.

"We have some people who left the Milford area who were prominent in town at the time. We have about a dozen calls there. Shafer told me that the drapes you saw in the steamer trunk were imported from Italy and that there were horse hairs embedded in the inside of the trunk. One other thing. The coal chute for the furnace was bricked over, but it was wide enough for the carpet to slide from the outside into the coal bin."

"That's important?"

"Yes," I say after swallowing the rest of my wine. "A strong man could tip the carpet into the top of the coal furnace, and an unsuspecting person could help the killer drag the steamer trunk into the basement. We first thought that the killer needed an accessory to do both."

"You really think things through," he says.

"Actually, Emelina and I talked the scenarios through with Shafer and Barney."

"They are making nice?"

"We are ahead of them and are turning over our cards as they turn over one for us. Erin would call this a separate and concurrent investigation. We are not working with them, and they aren't working with Milford's older version of Nancy Drew."

"I always had the hots for her," Ken says.

"How about the older version?"

"Definitely."

Talking time is over. We gently lift Billy from the couch and the three of us go upstairs, he to his crate and us to our bed.

Ken comes downstairs in the morning to a cheddar cheese omelet with a side of bacon and rye toast breakfast. He tells me about his day with several handyman jobs that shouldn't be too hard. The Devlin mansion project is now just a fart in the breeze, as our Sicilian friends would say. He is doing what he normally does in the winter when it's too cold to work outside.

As he digs into his breakfast, I pour a second cup of coffee and tell him, "Besides those phone calls I told you about, I am going to the library to look through the newspapers back at the time the Bidwells went missing to learn who was doing oil deliveries. I have a meeting next Tuesday at the Historical Society to do some more digging into Milford Coal & Ice."

"You are not ready to say that their neighbor might have done this?"

"No. I am still fixated on who built the partition to hide the bodies. I can't see Murphy having the wherewithal to pull that off." Ken is completely up to date on the case. He's much more receptive now than when that bag of bones spilled out on his toes. "Erin is taking the digital newspapers searches further with some of the information we've learned from our interviews, so we aren't completely finished. After that, I won't have much more to do, other than handing everything over to Shafer and telling him good luck."

"At least Emelina will share most of her secrets with you," he says. I know he is talking about the baking now.

"She's a great teacher. She has me write down the ingredients list and then the instructions. We work side by side on two batches following the recipe. Then she watches me make the next batch and tells me what I did right and wrong. It is a fantastic way to learn. We will be going non-stop Sunday and Monday for the Chamber of Commerce party."

"Hey, I'm a member," Ken remembers.

"Stop by the Chamber and buy a ticket. You will get to sample almost all of her goodies."

"Maybe Grammy LeGrande can babysit the grandkids and Erin and Darren can go too," he says.

I tell him, "That's a great idea. Maybe he can pick up some more clients from Milford." Darren is a financial planner and wealth manager, specializing in transplants from the city who are looking to live in a quieter location with a slower pace of life. "I'll call Erin this morning after meditation and yoga." Glancing at the clock, I add, "I've gotta scoot. You have Billy as your helper today?"

"Yes, Mrs. Strong," he says, mimicking the sing-song way my kindergarten class would respond to me over the years.

None of the kids ever got the kind of hug or kiss I plant on my guy before running out the door.

I see my first robins of the year. A flock is working over the birdseed on the ground put out by my neighbor. Forget groundhogs seeing their shadows—my harbinger of spring is my first robin sighting. I know that mid-February is about right for them to show up around here, even though there is plenty of bad weather still in store for us.

The sunrise is spectacular, with a band of orange above the tree line across the river. The breeze is not cold. It must be a southern breeze. Soon the geese will be winging their way north.

As I walk to Abe's studio, I round the corner and see a familiar car parked in front. The headlights blink at me, and I approach from the passenger side along the sidewalk. The window rolls down and Detective Shafer asks, "Do you have a minute, Gwen?"

I didn't think we were on a first name basis. "Sure." I look inside the studio and see that everyone hasn't settled in yet. "Just for a minute."

"That's all it will take. Hop in."

His black SUV is warm, and I undo my scarf, remove my knit hat, and let my parka breathe.

"We had the son of a bitch," Shafer starts.

"Who?"

"Murphy. I ran him in our system. We had a felony warrant out on him. Some felony warrants never expire."

A lovely day just got darker. He doesn't want to be seen talking to me. This must be serious.

"It was a rape complaint," he adds.

"When?"

"June 30th, 1970. He must have gotten wind of it and flown the coop."

"That's probably when he began drifting south," I say.

"Yep." Shafer is none too happy with the prospect that a very bad man got started in his backyard. Never mind that Shafer hadn't even been born yet—he carries the badge of an organization that let Murphy slip away, so it's personal. "I talked to a guy in records who pulled the paper file first thing this morning. We haven't gotten back that far in digitizing them."

"And?"

"Murphy was dishonorably discharged from the Service. He

was accused by a German citizen of the same thing. She dropped the charges when the Army offered to send him back to the States."

"That explains why his DD-214 wasn't in the county archives," I say.

"Correct. No VA benefits for him. He wouldn't want his dishonorable discharge papers to be in the public record."

"Who accused him?"

He opened his brown folder tucked between the console and his seat. "Gloria Michaels."

"She goes by Gloria Kennedy these days," I say. I fog his windshield with a deep exhale.

"You know her?" He looks at me with raised eyebrows but recovers quickly. "By now, I shouldn't be surprised by anything you tell me, Mrs. Strong."

"I do know her. She was Antoinette's maid of honor."

"Holy moly," he says.

"I know."

"The attack happened about the time the steamer trunk was hidden behind the partition," he says.

"She's lucky she's alive," I say. "I can take you to her house if you'd like. She should be home."

"Please."

It feels natural to be riding with Shafer to interview Gloria today. I can introduce them, and we both can hear what she says. I debate telling him that Emelina let it slip to me that her nephew suspected Antoinette of having a boyfriend. By proxy I will keep her secret… for now.

Gloria opens the door, and her smile quickly fades as I introduce her to Detective Shafer, who tells her about the felony warrant that was never canceled. The authorities in Florida never got around to contacting the State Police when they arrested Murphy.

"I never should have said anything to you, Mrs. Strong," she says. Her anger grows as she learns that Murphy was tied to killings and more sexual assaults below the Mason-Dixon line. She hisses at Shafer, "Maybe your people should have taken me more seriously." She wags an arthritic finger at him. The wounds are deep and raw now. Her anger is reaching a boiling point. It's painful to hear her recall what happened that summer night, but Shafer is gentle with her. It comes out that she knew him before the attack.

"Oh my God," I mutter.

We wait. The tumblers click on the safe holding back her memories, and she slowly opens the vault. She tells us, "He worked with Antoinette."

CHAPTER TWENTY-FOUR

Erin brings my adorable grandchildren to the library at the appointed time. I tell her about the Chamber of Commerce party, and she is elated at the thought of getting dressed up for a semi-formal affair. Homeschooling children means not wearing a nice dress and heels. I can see the symptoms of cabin fever setting in. She needs quality time with other adults.

We work the microfilm machines. As locals, we get an hour each while a couple of genealogists tap their toes impatiently. Abe and Emelina take turns coloring with April when not helping us feed the photocopier. We discover two coal delivery companies and two oil delivery firms advertising back in the day. Em recognizes two of them. We will visit Borough Hall to find out who the owners were from the Trade Name books. Erin confirms that three are out of business, as the Secretary of State's office has no listing for them. One company is still delivering oil—Pileggi and Sons. Emelina taught the elder Pileggi, and I taught his son Eddy.

When the hour is over, we repair to an unused reading room. Caleb and Jesse are busy with reading assignments, while April wears headphones over her tiny ears as she watches her favorite dinosaur shows on the family iPad.

In a quiet voice, I tell Erin, Abe, and Emelina why I was not at meditation or yoga this morning. Erin is impressed that Shafer sought me out immediately. "He knows that you are holding pieces of the puzzle," she says. "You told him about Murphy, and he told you about the arrest warrant, and two minutes later, he is interviewing the complainant, whom you've already talked to."

I glance at Emelina before proceeding. "He doesn't know that Andrew suspected Antoinette may have had a boyfriend."

"Who?" Erin asks.

"Andrew was going to tell Chief Kenrick. That is when he disappeared." Then I look at Abe and Erin. "Shafer is focusing on Murphy. I can't blame him."

I wait for Emelina to tell them that she was sworn to secrecy by Andrew, but she sits calmly without giving any hints away. She has chosen to tell me only so much. It's up to her to decide if she wants to share Andrew's suspicions with Abe and Erin.

"But?" Abe asks.

"It's hard to imagine Murphy had the ability to dispose of both bodies in the basement and build the partition with Mardell's permission," I say.

"Do you think that Murphy attacked Antoinette and got her pregnant?" he asks.

Erin makes sure her children are not eavesdropping. "Antoinette got pregnant by Murphy. She is pregnant with another man's child. She now knows that she is fertile, and that Andrew is the reason they can't have children. She works at Milford Coal & Ice with Murphy. She tells him she is pregnant and that she is keeping the child. He kills her instead and makes her disappear. Then he kills Andrew to keep him quiet. About three months later, Murphy attacks Gloria, but she reports him."

"That doesn't change the timing of Antoinette's death and her placement in the basement six months later and the ability of Murphy to wall off the basement," I persist.

Erin is about to reply but is interrupted by Emelina. "I think you have solved it. I can live with the possibility that a sexual predator killed my niece and nephew. I appreciate all your hard work." She stands on unsteady feet and makes her way out of the room. We watch as she gathers her coat, scarf, and hat before shuffling out of the library.

Erin, Abe, and I look at each other. Their stunned faces must match my expression. I tell them, "She said 'I can live with the possibility that a sexual predator killed my niece and nephew.' I wouldn't be surprised if Shafer and Barney say the same thing."

"There would be no trial, as the killer was killed in prison where he was awaiting trial for the same type of crimes," Erin says.

"He can't argue his innocence and offer evidence," I say.

"What are you two saying?" Abe asks.

"We don't have to go any further," Erin says.

"She can live with this version of the story," I say. I roll those words around my mouth like bitter herbs in a light dressing.

"Instead of digging deeper to find the truth," Erin adds.

"Emelina told me that Andrew suspected a boyfriend and swore her to secrecy," I say.

"She wouldn't tell you?" Abe asks.

"I think Antoinette would have told Emelina if she had been raped by a co-worker," I add.

Erin teaches Caleb and Jesse arithmetic and can put two and two together rather quickly. "What Mom is saying is that no good will come from suspecting the boyfriend and damaging his reputation when she can live with a reasonable and plausible explanation we just discussed. Case closed."

"But not solved," he says.

"Exactly," we say.

We look at the photocopies on the table. They are getting

cooler by the minute. The leads they contain are getting colder. Emelina said to drop the case, but here we sit.

Abe says, "Suppose for a minute that the boyfriend is still alive. Are you saying that Emelina would rather not know the truth than involve the boyfriend?"

"She didn't tell Mom that Antoinette was pregnant and wouldn't tell her who Andrew suspected," Erin says.

"Until Johnny Murphy came up on our radar, she probably thought the boyfriend got Antoinette pregnant," I say.

"Fifty years go by thinking Antoinette left Milford because she was pregnant with another man's child and didn't want to tell her husband," Abe says.

"The boyfriend didn't go with her. Why care about his reputation if he left with her?" Erin replies.

"Because he didn't go with her," I say. "And because Antoinette never left town."

"Then, after all these years, she finds out what happened to them," he says.

"If Andrew suspected Johnny Murphy, Emelina would have said something to us sooner," Erin says.

"Agreed," I say.

"But she doesn't suspect the boyfriend of killing either one," Abe says.

"So, where are we?" I ask slowly.

"You are in the library, Grammy Strong," April answers me. Her headphones are off, and the iPad is blank. How long has she been listening?

I look to Abe and say, "You are welcome to come back to my house for peanut butter and jelly sandwiches."

"If Emelina asks us to stop investigating, I will abide by her wishes," he says.

"I can't disagree with you, Abe," I say, "But you can still have a sandwich."

He smiles. "I like your use of a double negative. That's not the same as agreeing with me."

CHAPTER TWENTY-FIVE

Erin and I focus on the kids during lunch. Her oldest, Caleb, gets the bread out of the fridge and Jesse, her middle child, works the peanut butter on one slice, while April squirts the jelly on the other. Caleb carefully cuts five sandwiches with a bread knife. I sprinkle the sweet potato and beet chips on the plates while Erin pours milk. We eat and listen to recollections of what the kids did that morning. Double murders and skeletons can wait until later. I think of how my father was such a great listener at the dinner table all those years when my birth mother was too depressed to even get out of bed. He was probably craving adult companionship after a hard day's work at the airfield he was assigned to, but instead he focused all his attention on his only child, getting her fed, bathed, and tucked in for the night.

Ken and I made the dinner table a place where both Wesley and Erin were free to talk about their day before the adults did. Erin was a chatterbox. It took some prodding for Wesley, but he always knew he could talk to us if he wanted to. It was only recently that he opened up about the difficulties of being one of the few non-white kids in school and why his personal life is complicated.

I went by myself to my birth mother's funeral in Jamaica a short while ago. I think that now that this case is over, maybe the family could take a short week to visit my half-sister Brenda and her kids. It's warm there and it's winter here. Sandy beaches and tropical breezes versus snow drifts and occasional Arctic blasts. I know what I want to do with the dog reward money now—maybe I could ask the Stillman brothers if they wouldn't mind bumping us up to first class as a gift for figuring out what really happened in their case.

I brush the crumbs from the table while Erin wipes down the counter. The kids load the dishwasher with their plates and glasses.

Neither Erin nor I feel compelled to scan the photocopies from the library into CaseSoft. I will get around to it later. The wind is out of our sails. I wouldn't say it was smooth sailing working this case, but my friend just dropped the anchor on us. Will Emelina change her mind? I doubt it.

I follow my clan out to Erin's minivan and give them all extra hugs and kisses, then walk back into an empty house. My chest has a hollow feeling in it. I think about the kindergarten kids for the first time since the New Year's recess. Their teacher, Christine Flaherty, is due to have her baby any day now. The grapevine has it that when she takes family leave, the school will hire a substitute rather than have me fill in. I am sure Mary Meade, the school superintendent, had her hands in that. The apple doesn't fall far from the tree as I have found out. I think of the students for the first time in a while. I've been so totally focused on sleuthing that I haven't had time to think about what I loved about teaching for thirty-five years.

This case ended abruptly with no sense of completion. It has to do with being on the chase for clues, being on the hunt for suspects, and then to be told thanks but no thanks, your services are no longer necessary. That is where my sense of emptiness comes from. "Forget it Jake, It's Chinatown."—the ending of that movie said it so eloquently.

Emelina's dramatic departure from the library left us all stunned. This afternoon was to be spent on the case. Now what?

I pace around, wondering what to do. I could get started on some house chores, but I nix that idea immediately.

I missed my morning meditation and decided to follow a guided meditation from an app on my phone. I settle into my favorite spot on the couch, then kick off my shoes and press play. The woman speaks in a low melodic monotone with soft background music.

I wake to the sound of my ring tone for Erin. It's "Take On Me" by A-ha. I glance at the clock on the mantel. It has been over two hours since the kiddos departed.

"Hello?" I slur.

"Mom, are you okay?"

I take a deep breath. "I sat down to meditate and must have fallen asleep. Sweetie, I've fallen asleep in meditation and yoga before, but never like this. I settled into a deep trance with no recollection of dreams or thoughts." Waking up to Erin's call, everything is settled, and I am at peace.

"How could you fall asleep after what Emelina did today? I can't let it go. I keep running everything through my mind."

"Maybe I just needed a reset," I tell her. "To be truthful, I think she's holding back a lot more, not just what she was sworn to keep secret. We've been looking outward and never at her for clues. She told us just enough to get started."

"That's what I wanted to talk to you about," she says. "I thought we could bang some ideas around."

I choose my words carefully. "Honestly, Erin, I can let it go, although I will miss working with you on this one. If she wants to let the cops pin the murders on Johnny Murphy, she must have a good reason."

"Just like that, you are ready to quit?" she challenges me.

"In New Haven, the cops got it wrong and a lot more people died until we learned who killed that girl twenty years ago."

"And your point?"

"Last fall, we figured out what really happened to Jake and Brian in the Stillman matter."

"I'm not getting what you're driving at, Mom."

"One case was cold, and the other was hot, but in both cases, people cared about the outcomes. They were parents, friends, and family members. You went to the memorial service for Antoinette and Andrew. There were a few mourners there, sure, but only Emelina really cared about what happened to them all those years ago. The killer is dead, I am almost sure of it. Some of the town's upper crust wanted us to stop poking around…"

Then I have a blinding flash of the obvious. So this is what deep meditation must be like.

"What were you going to say?" she asks.

"I agree with what you said at the library. Emelina wants us to stop because we will do more harm than good. She has enough pieces to solve the puzzle."

"How can you say that?" Erin doesn't want to quit. I can't blame her. She did a ton of work on this case, and we are getting closer to solving it.

"She sees the whole board clearly, while we are still stumbling around in the dark. She has her answers. Doesn't matter who gave them to her."

"Without knowing the whole story, we supplied her with the missing pieces and now she has the answers to solve the mystery and she doesn't need us anymore." She summarizes what I just said perfectly.

"That's about it, honey. We don't get to find out the rest of the story."

"And you can live with that?" My daughter is blowing off steam, but not necessarily at me.

"If we go further, we may hurt Emelina. I can walk away knowing that we helped her figure it out."

"That's a tough pill to swallow, Mom."

"There's one other thing, Erin," I say.

"What's that?"

"My friend and mentor of many years won't live forever. She must have a sense of that. Why else would she be telling me all her cookie recipes? If it makes you feel better, you can think that we are just setting this case aside for the time being and not putting it away."

"Promise?" she says uneasily.

"Promise."

CHAPTER TWENTY-SIX

This morning, Ken rises early and takes Billy outside for his business. The back door creaks open again, and I know what's coming next. The clicking of nails on hardwood floors, the soft padding on carpeted stairway treads, and then the tippy-tap along the hallway to our bedroom. My little guy leaps up and lands on our bed. I get kisses, then he does his thing by rubbing his back and head against my soft Afro. "Somebody is spoiled," I say.

He burrows under the covers and attaches himself to my side. Snuggle time. He wants to snooze some more on this cold wintry morning, but if we want to go to Abe's studio, we have to get moving in a few minutes. His breathing is long and slow. I think about yesterday's events and promise to check in with Dr. Watson.

Erin isn't ready to stop investigating, and my sleuthing sidekick doesn't have the benefit of a deep meditation to help her see things as they are. She is a master at juggling many tasks, but she doesn't always like change. Having Emelina tell us to stand down is not easy for her, and I want to make sure she is alright. I must admit that my first thoughts of the morning are to review the case status. If I am going to scan the library photocopies into CaseSoft, I may as well close the loop by going to Borough Hall for the Trade Name register.

Finishing that piece of unfinished business will not mollify my daughter, but it does acknowledge there is plenty of sleuthing left on this case. I tell myself that this extra work will assist Detective Shafer. I wonder how he will react when he finds out Erin and I are off the case. We will turn over everything we have after the party and wish him the best. If they go with Johnny Murphy as the perp—listen to me, using *perp* in a sentence—it will give the State Police a black eye for letting him escape jurisdiction fifty years ago, but at least there won't be any finger pointing at anyone on the job since the turn of this millennium.

I let Billy sleep as I ease myself out of a warm bed and make my way to the bathroom. A natural hair style is easy to care for and shortens the time to take a shower, and before he knows it, I am dressed and making the bed. He looks at me like I am committing a crime as I make him move from under the blankets.

Ken kisses me and points to the coffee pot before heading out. I pour a cup, preparing it the way I like, with a little cream and maple syrup. Then rye toast with butter for me. Billy is the expensive eater in the morning with a prescribed salmon and vegetable entrée.

After breakfast, Billy and I head outside. "How's my favorite daughter?" I ask Erin over the phone as Billy discovers all the new overnight smells on our walk to the studio.

"I'm your only daughter," she says. Our standard opening patter.

"And my adorable grandchildren?"

"Everybody's fine. Darren's got a big client presentation today. He calls the guy 'the big tuna.' He promised to call me as soon as he finishes."

"How big?"

"Enough to move a comma on our tax return."

"That's a big fish," I say. "So about yesterday, honey…"

"I didn't sleep real well last night, Mom, tossing and turning over with what Emelina did. I can choose not to agree with you, but I can live with it. It's not like I don't have enough stuff going on around here, and I have been slacking on my night gig for the FBI. I can get back to that tonight."

"I can't imagine how this case would have turned out without your help, baby."

"I liked working it, because I was working with you, Mom."

"Abe helped out big time. I will make sure to tell him that today."

"We are a good team, aren't we?" she asks.

"The best," I say. "One other thing I was thinking. I am going to scan the photocopies in and get the trade names for the coal and oil delivery people. That is something we can have done for Shafer when we turn over everything to him next week."

"Sounds great. Oops, gotta go, Caleb and Jesse are fighting over something silly."

I am not sure how much she heard. I will let her know the time and date we meet with Shafer after the holiday weekend.

We make our way into the studio. Abe is seated along the side wall facing the class. Cushions are filling up fast. Emelina is already seated near the front and is surrounded by others. She seems at peace and there is nothing in Abe's expression to say otherwise. I remember her passing out in this very room after I showed her the necklace, Abe asking me why I showed a one-hundred-year-old woman a photo of a skeleton.

I sit on my cushion. Billy finds his spot in the middle of my crossed legs and resumes napping.

Abe chimes the bell, invoking the merit of our practice, and as the last sounds of the bell taper off, I return to that first discussion with Emelina and replay every step taken with the benefit of hindsight and knowledge that she knew more than she let on. Rather than being a discoverer of facts, she was confirming what she already knew, except for that part about Johnny Murphy. She was genuinely surprised about him and then what happened to Gloria Michaels Kennedy. Maybe cops or detectives have this opportunity for introspection when they work the midnight shift or have a long boring drive to the state lab or headquarters, but I find it invigorating to sit and contemplate with a singular focus what we learned and how Emelina reacted to everything.

The bell sounds, and I am astounded that I just spent sixty minutes ruminating on the case. I may never learn the whole story. As I unwind my legs and Billy wakes up, I am left with a feeling that I have important clues from the work we already have done. That fuzzy something is floating on the edge of my consciousness. Will I recognize it if I see it again? Will that piece explain the rest of puzzle?

We move the cushions to the side of the room and bring out the mats, bolsters, and blankets. I am not ready yet to let go of that fleeting feeling that I uncovered something and it's staring me in the face. I glance over at Emelina during triangle pose and know that she has that piece of the puzzle. We moved into our final pose, and I do not fall asleep for a change and keep going over all the interactions she had with people in this investigation. I think about those times when she cut people off. I first assumed it was from inexperience, but now I am wondering if it was something else to it.

Class is over. Abe, Emelina, and I move into the kitchen. There is no further discussion of the case. That ship has sailed. Em is ready to talk about the ingredients we need to buy today and tomorrow for Sunday and Monday's marathon baking. I am tasked to visit the big box stores on the edge of town for the lard, butter, three kinds of flour, and all kinds of sugar and salt, all purchased in bulk. This is not just for the Chamber of Commerce order but for us to fill up the pantry and refrigerator. We are kicking off Emelina's still unnamed business by taking in all these supplies. My mentor is serious about this venture and teaching me to bake.

She and Abe will visit some the local stores in town for artisanal supplies, unique or specialty items. She is going from here to the bridal shop to look at the cookie towers they rent for wedding receptions for ideas. Abe's itching to use his Amazon Prime card to buy some for her. We head off in our different directions as if there were no unsolved murders of her family members in this town. I look at my friend and mentor with different eyes now. At some point, I will learn what she knows, and I will make her confirm it for me.

Sir William and I make our way to Borough Hall. I use the excuse of checking on his dog licensing to have him with me. The clerks take turns giving him treats while I scan the Trade Names.

Milford Coal & Ice is a subsidiary of Bloodstone Industries. B. Bloodstone was the name to call for a delivery, according to the photocopies we made yesterday. Burgess Bloodstone is the CEO of the corporation, so that makes sense. We knew about Pileggi and Sons. I see Ken's name and his company. The clerk makes an exception for me and allows me to use my phone to pop a photo. The owner of A-1 Oil Delivery is Lawrence Kenrick. The other coal delivery company is Straub's Coal, and the owner is Wayne Straub. I don't recall teaching any Straubs, and I am not about to ask Emelina. I spend a whopping four dollars for the certified copies of the trade certificates for all the companies.

Ken meets me for lunch. There is no talk of homicide or bones hidden in a basement. He has two small jobs on this Friday afternoon, and he takes Billy with him. I feed each piece of paper from yesterday and today into my copier/fax/scanner and send it to Erin for entry into CaseSoft with the correct tagging. I go outside to my car to warm it up. I want to get out to the stores before people start their holiday weekend shopping. There is one last thing I will do before buttoning up the Bidwell case. I make a call.

"Hi, Mr. Sweet, this is Gwendolyn Strong. I spoke with you a little while ago about your days on the Milford Police Department."

"Make it quick Mrs. Strong. I'm on my fishing boat leaving the channel down here in Clearwater. I will lose cell service any minute.'

"A-1 Oil Delivery is the name of the company that Chief Kenrick's brother owned." I say that as a statement of fact.

"Yep, that's the one. I haven't heard that name in thirty years. They went out of business a couple three years after I quit the PD."

"Thank you, Tim." I don't think he hears me. He is out of cell range.

CHAPTER TWENTY-SEVEN

"My mother's mother gave me these recipes and I want to share them with you," Emelina tells me. "They were her mother's recipes from the old country. Over time, I've added some of my own."

Emelina knows every recipe by memory, and she is patient with me as I write down ingredients and baking instructions. She has already figured out what order we will follow and which ovens we will use. Over the next two days, we are going to make three dozen each of twenty-four specialty cookies. On top of that, every attendee with get a take-home box of the assortment, which will include her prized chocolate chip cookies.

It is as if the last couple of weeks working on Antoinette and Andrew's murders never happened. My new gig is starting today, and it takes all my concentration. Em is patient with my mistakes and makes gentle corrections before things go into the oven. She makes a batch. I watch. Then she watches me make a batch and we taste the two. She is the wine connoisseur of cookies, and in the side-by-side comparisons, I begin to tease out the subtle differences. We find out we need extra pans and trays, and we need them rather quickly. I take photos of them. I bribe Ken to go to the store to buy them. My guy flies into the kitchen in record time with the merchandise. We fawn over him as he goes from spicy ginger molasses to applesauce raisin chews to lemon pecan. The man is higher than a kite on sugar by the time we send him home. Make, bake, wash, repeat. Next are peanut butter oatmeal treats, apple cider cookies, drop sugar cookies. They all have her little signatures and variations that make the flavor pop in my mouth. Time, temperature, and handling all are explained by Emelina, and I take copious notes. We are learning the ovens as well. Viennese hazel butter thins, date pinwheel cookies, and a variation on chocolate and peanut butter are next. The time flies.

We finish the day with vanilla butter crescents, chocolate almond buttons, and honey carrot cookies. Emelina is a stickler about cleaning everything and wiping the surfaces down. All the bowls, pans, cookie cutters, and utensils are hung up. Everything is spotless. Except for the smells permeating the air, you wouldn't know that we baked eighteen dozen cookies today. I learn more in eight hours than I could from a lifetime of watching the baking shows.

We close up the studio just before dark and walk our separate ways home. There was no idle chit-chat today between rounds and certainly no talk of the murders which have consumed our attention since the day after Ken literally stumbled upon Antoinette's remains.

In the fading twilight, my thoughts settle on my future. If I had a choice between baking with Emelina all the time or sleuthing with Erin, which would it be? I question why it has to be an either-or scenario. For now, it must be. Emelina Bidwell is my baking partner in the real sense of the word, and she no longer requires my other non-teaching skills. Will there be a void until the next case comes along? There, I said it to myself. There will be a next case, but as soon as I think it, clarity after stepping away for two days from the forest that was the speculation about the twin killing from fifty years ago allows me to see the trees.

Working with sugar and spice and everything nice today and giving it my fullest concentration allows me space to rethink some of our previous operating assumptions. Again, clues surface on the periphery of my consciousness, dancing like the twinkling stars over the river on this moonless night. They feel close enough to touch, but as my granddaughter Jesse would tell me, they are millions of miles away. I am not comforted that the clues are much closer, but as elusive to touch. C'mon, Captain Obvious, throw me a bone.

My little guy greets me with his whole body wagging before my big guy gives me a hug and peck.

Ken looks perplexed. "No extras?"

"Sorry, honey. They are all accounted for."

"How many did you make?"

"Eighteen dozen. We have the same amount to make tomorrow."

"How did it go?"

"Emelina is a great teacher, but we already knew that. She was patient with me. I watched her make a batch and then she watched me. She's a perfectionist but without dinging me for mistakes. Now, if I make the same mistakes tomorrow, it might be a different story."

He surprises me by saying, "I was thinking more about your case."

"Not a single word was said. We had some downtime between bakes while we were cleaning pots and pans, but she didn't bring it up."

"Strange," he says.

"Why do you say that?"

"You are working side by side all day and don't talk about all the things you did together for the last couple of weeks. I don't get it, especially because it involved the biggest news to hit Milford since, well, your last two cases."

"She knows more than she's telling us, hon," I say. We move into the kitchen. He helps by setting the table, while I stir the crock pot. Beef stew. "Erin and I think that we unwittingly gave her the last pieces of the puzzle. She can see the whole picture, but we can't."

"How does that make you feel?"

"She's entitled to her privacy. We will turn everything over to Detective Shafer after the party and let him run with it. She can't stop him from investigating two murders, even if they happened over fifty years ago."

He smiles at me. "What is it you always say to me? Thank you for your response but can you answer the question?"

"Ken, you are asking me about those squishy things? You know, what do you call them?"

"Feelings?"

"Yeah, those things. You know how good I am at burying them deep down inside."

"Are any bubbling to the surface?"

"Nope. At first, I was shocked by how she just walked out on us, but then I came to understand that she got what she needed."

"Which was?"

"A reasonable explanation to what happened. Johnny Murphy killed Antoinette to keep her quiet about a possible rape and ensuing pregnancy with his child and then killing Andrew, who might have figured it out."

"But you don't think that is the case, do you?"

"I don't see how a coal delivery guy can hide both bodies by building a partition wall."

Ken thinks about that as he feeds Billy. I start to ladle out the stew into our bowls.

I say, "My friend of over thirty-five years discovers what

happened to her niece and nephew, and it was not from her receiving a couple of postcards from Hawaii. They were found murdered and stuffed in a trunk and a coal furnace shortly after they went missing. Her world gets turned upside down. Then we figure out what might have happened, and it fits with what she already thinks but wasn't telling us. I can't beat her up for wanting to halt my snooping. I guess I feel compassion for her. I can't let my need to solve the mystery get in the way of that." We move to the kitchen table. Neither of us reaches for our soup spoons. Ken is waiting for me to finish rummaging around for those squishy things, just as much as I am trying to verbalize them.

"Do you remember that time when we were dating," I say to him, "and we were in my parent's basement, and we heard the upstairs door open?" Ken and I had been going out together for a while at that time, and this wasn't our first time to the rodeo. "We were very much in the moment and then everything came to an immediate halt."

He grins at me. "It feels like that?"

"Worse."

CHAPTER TWENTY-EIGHT

"Thank you all for coming tonight," Benjamin begins his speech. "On behalf of the Milford Chamber of Commerce, I welcome you to the Annual Membership Drive." He looks dapper in his blue suit, starched white shirt, and magenta tie. There is a sparkle in his eyes, and his energy is contagious.

He strategically waited until after the endless platters of hors d'oeuvres and an hour of open bar to make his pitch. The businesspeople of our fair town have been fed and are nicely lubricated. It's our signal to bring out the cookies and fill the towers. Emelina and I strike a balance. She dresses nicely, while I am the worker bee. I scurry between the three serving tables next to the drink stations, making sure every table has an equal measure of our tasty creations, while she follows behind me and lifts off the cling wrap and tidies each arrangement.

Benjamin continues, "As our economy continues to evolve, I am happy see so many new faces. If this is your first visit to a Chamber event, please raise your hand." I see Erin and Darren raise their hands, along with a couple dozen other folks. My daughter and son-in-law are with Ken, who bought a new suit for the occasion. "Let's show these folks a round of applause and a hearty welcome." He pauses for the desired effect. "Milford was first known for logging, and after the river was tamed, industry grew up along its banks using hydro-electric power for the mills and for building barges to send our goods downstream. The railroads came next with reliable freight transportation and with it, summer tourism."

Here in the Bloodstone mansion, which now houses a museum of Commerce and Industry, the examples are all around me. A weaving mill that was used to make Union Civil War uniforms sits in the center of the main hall. Along the walls are exhibits and photo displays of progress over the years. The displays stop in the 1950s.

He continues, "One thing is certain, and that is change. Did we try to hold on the past?" He looks about the room, and his eyes settle on the life-size portrait of his father, Burgess. The unsmiling face and stern countenance say it all about trying to hold onto the good ol' days.

"Sadly, yes, but from this experience, we had to learn to be nimble. Farming today is organic. City folks cannot get enough of our produce. We raise the best beef, pork, and poultry without all the nasty stuff. Our grand hotels have little vacancies now as year-round bed and breakfasts. Many restored Victorian mansions are Airbnb's. Can I have a show of hands of business owners of health and wellness studios?" A dozen hands go up in the air. "Please keep your hands in the air. As I call your type of business, raise your hand, and keep it up."

"But even with this rebirth, we cannot do it without our tradespeople, craftsmen, construction and heavy equipment operators. Also, our financial service sector of insurance, accounting, banking, and legal services." I watch as a coven of lawyers and bankers raise their hands. "You can buy a car and have it serviced here in Milford. Downtown has a near one hundred percent occupancy rate with artisanal retail." More hands go up. "We even have a yoga studio." Abe raises his hand sheepishly. "And a brand-new bakery. Your dessert tonight is supplied by our one and only Emelina Bidwell." I have never seen her turn red before—he caught her completely unawares.

"Before you put your hands down, only lower them if you haven't used a Chamber discount in the last couple of years." Only a few hands drop. "Look around." He pauses. "Besides discounts, we have four leads groups, in-house training seminars on business start-ups, and lobbyists working at the state capital to promote our state and our town as a place to relocate a business."

He's winding down now. "Okay, you can put your hands down now, but before you reach for one of Emelina's prized cookies, find a hand of a new person tonight and shake it. Introduce yourself and ask them what they do. Let them know how valuable your membership is to your business. Enjoy the evening, everyone."

It's one the of best speeches I've ever heard. Short, sweet, and to the point. Some of the preachers in town could learn from him. I am happy for Benjamin, and I am happy for Emelina and our new venture. It feels real to me tonight as I see people I've known all my adult life mingling with new folks in town.

"Excuse me, miss. May I have a napkin?" I turn to see Truscott Daniels. "Oh, I didn't recognize you, Mrs. Strong, I thought you were one of the servers."

He might as well have called me a servant. I am still processing his insult when from over my shoulder I hear, "Here you go, Daniels, it's a shame you spilled your drink on your tie."

Ken's strong hand pushes a handful of napkins towards Daniels' drink hand, causing it to do just that.

"You—" Truscott's anger flashes for a second. "Be careful."

"You be careful too, counselor." My man gives him a tight thin-lipped smile.

Daniels turns away and slinks to the corner where his ilk have camped out. Erin, Darren, and Abe join Ken and me. We have enough for a rugby scrum. Milford's power elite versus Milford's truth seekers. This one could leave scars.

The mumbling and harrumphing fade as Truscott and the others scatter around the hall.

I know someone who is going to get help with taking his clothes off tonight. My man gives my middle back a gentle pat. He always has my back. I take a deep breath and refocus on making sure the displays are well stocked. Then I walk back to the kitchen and see Emelina and Benjamin. They are in a tender embrace. I cough.

He lifts his head, and she turns around and says, "I was just filling him in with the news about Johnny Murphy."

"So, your investigation is over," Ben says. "That was some amazing work."

"Yes, we are going to turn everything over to the authorities tomorrow," I say.

I grab the next platter and whoosh out the door. You would think this group was a pack of ravenous wolves. The serving tables are nearly empty. The compliments I am receiving only validate what I already know. This get-together is the launch party for Emelina's cookies, and she has achieved lift-off. No sooner do I empty that tray when I spot another totally barren tower. I rush back to the kitchen to grab the next platter and hear Emelina sobbing. I walk over to her and put my arms around her. She says, "This is supposed to be a happy occasion, and here I am falling apart."

"I'm sure that talking to Benjamin allowed you to finally grieve your niece and your nephew. Grief can come when you least expect it." I put my arms around her and give her a hug. I think of all the times that she has hugged me over the years. Those times when I wanted to commit a felony against the school principal or administrator, or squabbles with Ken over whether to medicate Erin when her teachers were demanding it, Em was always there for me. Maybe I am not the greatest at verbalizing my feelings, but she always seemed to know when I needed a hug. Now, it's my turn. "Your cookies are a big hit. They can't get enough," I say.

"Maybe we should bring out the goody boxes after that last platter," she says. "Let's send them home happy."

I had suggested that we put a label on her boxes with a website and her telephone number and she agreed to just her telephone number for now. Each to-go box has a nice hand-printed label with her name and telephone number.

Mayor Scudder approaches me. "Good evening, Mrs. Strong. How are you?"

"I am well, Mr. Mayor."

"These cookies are fantastic. I am glad that Emelina decided to do this. I am sure you had a hand in all this."

"Matter of fact, we are partners."

He seems surprised by that statement. "Anyway, this is a nice way to put all that unpleasant business behind you."

The grapevine has fiber optic speed in this town. "Yes sir, two unsolved homicides from fifty years ago in town would definitely be unpleasant." I hold the politician's stare longer.

"Congratulation on a wonderful new business venture. I know who to call for our business functions."

He's slick. He's slicker than snail stuff, but I return his fake smile before he steps away.

Erin comes back to the kitchen. She's little tipsy. We Strongs are not big drinkers, but it's a rare night out for her, and Darren's her designated driver. She looks great in a slinky black dress that accentuates her curves. I know where she got those from. "Do you need help with anything, Mommy?" she asks.

"I know a couple guys' drinks you could spike," I say.

She looks under the sink at the cleaning products. "Death or just diarrhea?" I am not sure if she's joking.

"No, your dad put one of them in his place."

"Well, after what Daniels did to Daddy, I think he owed him one."

"Tru dat," I say, borrowing a phrase that our favorite FBI agent, Marsha O'Shea, said during the New Haven case.

"What was Emelina upset about?" Erin doesn't miss a trick.

"She told Mr. Bloodstone about Johnny Murphy, and I guess it all came crashing down on her tonight," I say. "She told him that our investigation is finito."

"I guess that's it," she says. "It was fun while it lasted."

"Are you coming with me tomorrow afternoon to see Detective Shafer?" I ask.

She nods. "Wouldn't miss it for the world. We get to show a homicide investigator how it's done," she says, giggling.

"Will you have everything ready?" I ask.

She nods. "You can give him the dossiers and I will put everything else on a thumb drive. I can't give him access to CaseSoft, as it's not ours to share in the first place."

My turn to nod. "Makes sense. Do you want to help me with the goody boxes?"

"They are so cute, but how come you didn't create a social media page or a website?"

"Emelina nixed that idea, so we just went with her phone number."

"That's so old school, Mom," she says as we load the boxes onto a serving cart.

"She's a hundred years old, Erin."

"Yeah, but look how she picked up on how we worked the case. She could kill it on TikTok."

I roll my eyes at her. "Really, Erin?"

"Really, Mom. People would pay good money all over the world to try her chocolate chip cookies."

I can't argue with her. Guests are coming to us, and we can't hand them out fast enough. I have to tell people politely that they only get one box. I save two for Ken. He can have Daniels' take home.

The bar has been closed for a while and people are making their way to the exits. I huddle with Emelina one more time. Abe has offered to give her a ride home. He says, "Your cookies are a success."

"Our cookies are a success," she says, then she gives me a hug. "Thank you for everything, Gwendolyn. I truly mean that."

I know she's talking about the case and not Chinese chews or magic cookie bars.

My chariot driver appears, and we stroll outside to his truck. Except for Truscott Daniels putting me down, it was a wonderful evening. It's cloudy tonight, but not frigid.

Spring is coming. I can feel it. I am ready to say sayonara to Old Man Winter. The parking lot is deserted except for us and an SUV tucked in the darkened corner of the parking lot facing outwards.

We depart and are chatting about Ken's favorite cookies. He can't decide between his old favorite and some of the ones we baked today.

We are halfway home and turning off the main drag when the inside of our cab is lit up by blue and red flashing strobes. The police vehicle and our car are the only ones on the road. Ken slows down to allow it to pass. We figure the officer is heading to an emergency. Instead, it tucks in behind us and throws its searchlight on our sideview mirror. We are being stopped.

"Did you have much to drink tonight?" I ask.

"No more than anybody else," he replies.

The laws are so strict these days, you can look at a bottle of beer and get pinched for a DUI.

We are blinded by the lights reflecting back in our eyes from the mirrors A shadow cuts the light, and the police officer approaches the driver side window. Ken eases it down. An oversized flashlight sweeps the interior of our passenger compartment.

"May I see your driver's license, registration, and proof of insurance?"

It's Barney Williams.

"Barney, this is my husband, Ken." I say.

He says nothing in response. What's going on?

Ken leans across me and retrieves the registration and insurance card from the glove box. He also produces his driver's license and hands everything over.

"Thank you, sir. I will be right back."

The search light stayed focused on the rearview mirror. The blue and red lights continue to strum a strobe effect over the empty street and houses on both sides of this neighborhood street.

"Daniels got to Scudder and Scudder got to Barney." I shake my head. Next, I expect him to ask Ken to take a field sobriety test, then watch him go in handcuffs to the State Police Barracks for a breathalyzer. He may be over the limit and could go to jail. I am starting to think the car I saw in the parking lot was Barney's police vehicle. This is a trap. I am getting more perturbed by the minute.

I can't believe this. I have the Stillman brothers' attorney on speed dial. I am tempted to call now while we sit here helpless to leave.

Eventually Barney ambles up to the window and hands Ken's papers back to him. "Thank you, Mr. Strong. Have a nice evening."

"What the—" I say. Is he doing this just to harass us?

He walks back to his ride, turns off the overhead lights and searchlight, then drives away swiftly.

Ken takes his license and puts in back in his wallet. I take the papers and am ready to put them back when I notice a third piece of paper. I put the insurance ID card and his registration back in the glove box and stare at the remaining piece. I unfold it and get it oriented so I can read it.

"What's that?" Ken asks. His adrenaline is bleeding off.

"I think that was all a ruse. Barney wanted to give me this while making it look like a routine traffic stop. It's a photocopy of the Milford Jailer's intake card. It shows Johnny Murphy spent Christmas Eve and Christmas day 1969 in the pokey for drunk and disorderly until Mrs. Murphy bailed him out."

"I don't get it."

"Andrew said Antoinette went missing after dinner and before Midnight Mass on Christmas Eve. Murphy couldn't have grabbed her then."

CHAPTER TWENTY-NINE

It's noon. Erin is looking a little haggard. Drinking during the week doesn't agree with her. Grammy LeGrande is watching our adorable grandchildren again. She is a wonderful woman, and I am grateful that my daughter married into this family. The weather turned cold overnight, and it looks like Old Man Winter is giving us the single digit salute. He can't decide whether to pelt us with snow, sleet, or freezing rain today. The roads are a mess, and Erin's drive was slowed by accidents and jack-knifed tractor trailers. She phones me enroute that she will be running late. Her minivan is like a tank and can plow through anything, but even today she is shaken by the drive. She makes our appointment with Karen Manilla at the Historical Society with just minutes to spare. "Sorry, Mom. Traffic was horrendous. You would think people would know how to drive in this stuff by now."

"Just glad you made it safe. Not sure if we are going to find anything more here, but it's worth a shot," I say. "Did you get what I asked for?"

"Megan Murphy is now Megan Burt, and she lives in Pleasant Valley. Here is her cell number."

"You're the best," I tell her as we walk from the slushy parking lot to the clapboard Victorian.

Erin continues, "She was married at the time of her mother's death, and I found her in Mrs. Murphy's obituary."

"Maybe she can tell us about that Christmas of 1969 with her brother Johnny."

We wipe the moisture from our boots and enter the warmth of the Historical Society. Karen is waiting for us. "Good morning, Gwen."

"Good morning, Karen. This is my daughter Erin."

"Nice to meet you."

"Likewise," Erin replies.

"I am sorry to say we didn't have anything specific to Milford mansions. You could scroll through the society page of the papers on microfilm at the library. They ran features on Sunday mostly."

"That's a good tip." I say. Secretly, I know that won't happen. When we are done here today, we are done. I didn't even tell Emelina about this trip. Quite frankly, I had forgotten about this appointment until Karen called me this morning asking me if I still wanted to come in due to the weather. Erin begged me to come, and she got everything together for our meeting with Shafer later this afternoon in record time. My daughter is not ready to leave this case alone, and with the revelation that Murphy was not out and about when Antoinette Bidwell went missing, she is ready to jump back on the saddle again. That's the other thing I didn't tell Emelina about. I purposely blew off yoga this morning to avoid her.

Karen continues, "More bad news. I couldn't find much on Milford Coal & Ice, but I did learn that it was owned by Bloodstone Industries, so I pulled everything on that and on the Bloodstones. I went back as far as the mid-1930's. Did you know that Benjamin Bloodstone is the president of the Chamber of Commerce?"

"Yes, we do."

"I went to school with Benny. We were in school plays together. He's such a nice fellow. I always wondered why he never married."

We smile. We don't engage her with this little piece of personal trivia. Both Erin and I are fixated on the boxes in front of us on the large conference table.

"We did come through on your last request," Karen continues. "Here are all the photos taken in 1969 and 1970 by both papers. I had forgotten that they were not just the photographs that appeared in the papers, but also of all the photos that were developed from the roll. You are going to have some fun this afternoon, getting a snapshot of Milford during that era."

"Thank you, Karen. This is wonderful. You did a great job." I say it and I mean it. Thinking back to how Vickie Scudder found the index cards responsive to my FOIA request, she could have easily told Barney there were no reports and she would have been correct. You are at the mercy of the people that work in records rooms, repositories, or archives, and you treasure diggers and abhor clock punchers. Like Forrest Gump's box of chocolates, you never know what you are going to get.

After she leaves us to our work, I say to Erin, "Thank goodness you are with me. Two papers with two years of photos, along with forty years of clippings about one of Milford's most prominent families, is more than an afternoon's work for one person.

"What did Casey McFadden use to say?" Erin is referencing the cold case homicide detective brought out of retirement by the New Haven PD to work with FBI agent Marsha O'Shea.

"Ain't nothing to it but to do it," I reply.

About an hour into our research, Erin comes up for air first. "These Bloodstones are hard men. Benjamin's grandfather makes his father look like an altar boy. It was tough sledding for them during the Depression, but they kept mushing and were rewarded with military contracts during World War II. Then in the post-war years, their manufacturing really took off into the mid-1960s. Burgess wasn't expecting foreign competition from Mexico or Japan and their empire shrunk in the 1970s. His op-eds in the afternoon paper railed for better trade agreements and protectionist tariffs. He was one bitter hombre. He was born into wealth and affluence and watched as his status in the community shrank. He was angry at the war protests and complained to the Chamber of Commerce that he lost out on government work to companies down South with cheaper labor."

"Emelina told me that he acted like a big shot. He had a brand-new Cadillac every year and ran the country club with an iron fist," I say.

She holds up the final articles and tells me, "I will start helping you with the photos in about fifteen minutes."

"Good, I need to stretch and take a break. I am going out on the porch for some fresh air and to try reaching Megan Burt." Flipping photos with no real purpose has lulled me into an afternoon's sluggishness.

I throw on my coat, head outside, and realize how warm Karen keeps the Society. The blast of freezing air wakes me up immediately. I dial Megan Burt and she answers. I explain the purpose for my call.

"Yeah, I heard about them finding the Bidwells like that," she says. "That was awful. Especially that poor girl, she deserved better in life. All this time, we thought she got away from her husband."

"Andrew?"

"Yep. Before she split, well we thought she split, he was slapping her around pretty regularly."

"You are the first to mention that to us."

"We were neighbors, we could hear everything. Nobody ever called the cops back then. You minded your own business."

"Yes, that was before my time," I say with a neutral tone.

"She was such a sweet girl. She got Johnny a job where she worked. Did you know that? He really liked working there."

"Milford Coal & Ice?"

"Uh-huh. He did deliveries. He wasn't stuck in some factory somewhere."

"So, I have to ask you about Christmas 1969." I've warmed her up, and she doesn't mind talking with me as long as I avoid what her brother became and how he died.

"Johnny did some charity event at work, and they did such a good job, the boss gave them Christmas Eve off. Well, he started drinking at their holiday party and kept it up at home. He was in good spirits. Best I saw him in a long time. Then we heard Andrew yelling at her and for the first time she yelled back at him. Well, I guess he didn't like that and really laid into her. My mother told Johnny to mind his own business, but he went over there anyway and set Andrew straight. He didn't say what he said or did, but after midnight the cops showed up and dragged Johnny to jail. The jerk must have called the cops on him. Go figure. My brother goes next door to stop a man from beating his wife and he gets arrested."

"I see." This is the best I can muster.

"My mother was really mad at Johnny and left him to sit in jail over Christmas. She told him not to get involved. We had to come up with bail money and a lawyer. My mother, God rest her soul, said that money didn't grow on trees. She said that all the time."

"And Antoinette?"

"We didn't see her again. We thought she left Andrew. Couldn't blame her. She didn't do nothing to deserve being his punching bag. A couple months later, the guy splits too and leaves the house vacant."

"What did you think happened when you found out what really happened to Mr. and Mrs. Bidwell?"

"Andrew killed her and then somebody killed him."

"Are you thinking that somebody was Johnny?"

"No comment, Mrs. Strong." An informative conversation ends with a click. I could have handled that last part better. I gaze out at the snow. It's snowing harder now and it's sticking.

I am freezing, but my temper is heating up. I walk inside and sit across from Erin with my hands stuffed in my parka.

She looks up from an eight by ten glossy photo and asks with an alarmed gaze, "What's wrong, Mom?"

"Blood is thicker than water." I relate my call and am happy that Emelina is nowhere in sight. She would get an earful from me. Partner, mentor, friend be damned. I don't like being played.

Erin listens without interrupting, and after I blow more steam off, she says, "A couple of things don't make sense. How would Murphy know that Andrew killed her and then put both their bodies behind the partition?"

"I agree. And the other thing," she continues. "I've just spent a lot of time reading about the Bloodstones, and Benjamin's father would not sponsor a charity or give his people a day off. I can guarantee you that."

"Johnny Murphy as a good guy? How does that play with you?"

"We only have his sister's word for it," Erin replies.

"What about Andrew beating Antoinette?"

"Neighbors hear and see things. I find that credible, and that is why Megan thought Antoinette left Andrew."

"Antoinette tells Emelina that she is pregnant, has a boyfriend, but omits that Andrew is abusing her regularly."

"I can see why you are incensed, Mom. Emelina is playing us. Do you think that Murphy is the father?"

"And that he didn't assault her either?" I add.

"Yes," Erin says.

"Hard to believe it, but I find Megan credible and think that Johnny Murphy could be the boyfriend and the father," I say.

We split up the rest of the photos from 1969. What are we looking for? Emelina is no longer reliable, and I have to wonder if we have anything left to accomplish. Is there a needle in this haystack of professional photographs? And would I recognize the needle even if I saw it? We have a couple of hours before we meet Shafer, and it's warm and cozy here. Might as well run out the string.

I am looking at Thanksgiving feature photos and see a reenactment with persons dressed as Pilgrims and Native Americans. I am holding the photograph and feel I am not seeing something. It reminds me of those clues which appear just out of focus, like the snowflakes outside the frosty window.

I take a deep breath and return to the photos. My eyes focus on the scenes in the roll not used for print. It takes me a second. I look at the description on the backs and flip back to the glossy black and white images. Suddenly, everything comes into focus. "Erin! I found something." I slide the photo across the table.

She stares at it, then at me. She nods, seeing how this puzzle piece fits too.

I look back at the photograph. "We have time for one more interview before we see Shafer, don't you think?" I look closer at the Thanksgiving photograph and now I recognize two of the pilgrims.

CHAPTER THIRTY

"Is this one of the last times you saw her alive?" I ask. In the photo, Antoinette is flanked by two men. They are standing behind heaps of coats. The caption reads, *Milford Coal & Ice Coat Drive, December 23rd, 1969.* The other man in the photo is a smiling Johnny Murphy.

Benjamin Bloodstone nods his head while fingering the photo Erin discovered. We've "borrowed" it from the Historical Society for this show and tell. We decided that I will do the showing and the telling. No more asking.

"This is you and her too." I slide the other "borrowed" photograph across his desk.

He smiles at the memory of the Thanksgiving reenactment, but his sadness returns quickly.

"You were her boyfriend."

"Yes," he says.

"She was pregnant with your child."

He nods again.

"You were just as surprised as Emelina when she recognized the necklace, she had given Antoinette.

"Yes."

"And you knew immediately who killed her."

"Yes."

"And then later, you figured out who killed Andrew." I am reaching here, but I am on a roll.

He nods.

Once we saw the photos, the who came into focus, the motive is a little bit trickier.

"After Andrew beat her that last time just before Christmas, you agreed that she could no longer live with him."

He nods.

"But your father objected, didn't he, Ben?"

The office of the president of the Chamber of Commerce overlooks Milford's main intersection. There are awards on the walls and photos of him with governors and captains of industry. His desk is not ornate, but it is an antique. Our chairs are pulled up close and we decide not to make notes or record the conversation. Erin had closed the door behind her before we told him why we wanted to see him. This man, who led the festivities the night before, is not prepared for this conversation but has been waiting for it since the day my husband discovered the skeletons of his lover and his lover's husband.

"My father told me that Antoinette had trapped me into getting her pregnant and that she didn't love me. She only wanted my money. His money. He asked me what I knew about love. I had only been out of graduate school for a few years. He appointed me as the sales manager for Milford Coal & Ice. That is where I met Antoinette. She was our bookkeeper."

We all sip from our coffees before he continues. "She liked movies and plays. She read every adventure and mystery book she could take out of the library. She was a dreamer. We had so much in common, unlike the man she had married. I supposed they loved each other at one time, but he was hell bent on crushing her spirit."

"And you nourished her spirit," I add. I need him to keep reminiscing.

"When I wasn't making sales calls, it was just her and me in the office. We would play classical music on the radio and talk about what she was reading. I fell in love with her."

"And she fell in love with you. You were younger by about…"

"Seven years, but it didn't matter."

"Then she got pregnant. You knew it was your baby because she and Andrew had been trying for years and he blamed her for being infertile."

"After the last time he beat her, she was worried for the baby and decided to leave him. We would get married and start our family."

"But your father had other ideas."

"He told me that he met with her that Christmas Eve and gave her what she really wanted. He told me he gave her twenty thousand dollars in cash, but she had to leave and never come back. He told me no bastard child would take the Bloodstone name and become an heir to the family fortune."

"How did that make you feel?"

"I was livid. I couldn't believe he bought her off."

He looked out at the blizzard pummeling our town "I didn't hear from her. No calls at work, no postcards, nothing, Weeks went by, then months. One night I overheard my father talking with Chief Kenrick. Kenrick would take care of problems for my father, but it always came with a price tag. Andrew must have put two and two together. He wanted the police to start an investigation into her disappearance. He wanted the police to investigate me. Kenrick was a greedy SOB, but in the end, he took care of Andrew. We never heard from him again. I figured they bought him off too."

He thinks about what he says next and punctuates his thought with a deep exhale. "About six months after she left without a trace, my father asked me to help move a steamer trunk."

"I see where this is going."

"He said that Mardell wanted to buy some fancy drapes we had put in storage, but we had to move it for him. My father never did any physical labor, but we took it from our basement to his basement. Mardell wasn't even home. Chief Kenrick was helping his brother install an oil burner there at the time."

"And Andrew was already stuffed into the coal furnace."

"Apparently so. As time went by, I came to believe my father. It broke my heart to think that Antoinette only wanted our money. I expected to hear from her when the baby was born, but I heard nothing. As the years went by, my father would remind me how foolish I was."

We wait. This story was fifty years in the making.

His voice quivers. "I truly loved her. It was then I decided that I was not going to provide my father with heirs to the family fortune. I remained single and put all my energy into philanthropic projects and making Milford a better place to live. In the end, the old man sold off most our assets and created the trust. He died an angry bitter man, and I was happy to see him go. After he died, I thought Antoinette might come back to town, but by then she may have started a new life, gotten married, had more kids. Our town was in her rearview mirror."

"Did you ever suspect him of killing Antoinette?"

"Not until your husband stumbled across the trunk, I swear. A short time later, your husband found the skeleton shot in the head. I figured Kenrick kept the buy-off money and killed Andrew. He took care of the problem for my father and profited by it."

Former police officer Timothy Sweet's words now make more sense to me.

"When did you tell Emelina?" Erin asks.

"Two days after the funeral services."

"And you swore her to secrecy?" I ask.

"Yes."

"She is good at keeping secrets," I say. There will be time later to recall how Emelina's attitude changed towards the investigation after Bloodstone's revelation.

"What's next?" he asks.

"You come with us and tell Detective Shafer what you just told Erin and me," I say.

"And then what?"

"They check out your story and see if they can corroborate what you are telling them."

"Supposing they somehow can do that. Then what?"

"They solve both murders."

"Then what?"

"End of story," I say.

"Not necessarily," Erin says.

"What do you mean?" I ask her.

"Ask him," she says.

I look at Benjamin.

"Antoinette died first, and she was still married to Andrew, so technically, her estate would go to him," Benjamin says.

"Then he died without a will, so his estate would go to his nearest living relative," Erin says.

"That would be Emelina," I say. "But they didn't have any money. I'm confused."

"Mom, Burgess Bloodstone created a Trust, and he is liable for Antoinette's death and is partially responsible for Andrew's death, along with Herman Kenrick, who was approached by Andrew to investigate the disappearance of his wife and instead kills him. The Borough would be on the hook for his actions."

"The Borough has no money, and the Trust will spend every penny on fighting the allegations rather than admit liability. It would be years before Emelina or her beneficiaries would see a dime," Benjamin says.

"What if Emelina doesn't want to sue the Trust or the Borough?" I ask.

"By coming forward, the Trust, which supports almost all the charities in town, and the Borough would both get black eyes."

"That is why Daniels and Meade went to Mardell and warned the cops not to talk to me. You sent your attack dogs after my husband." I want to get angry with this man, but I can't.

"I've committed my life to making things better around here," he says, "both with the Trust and by working with the Chamber. Tell me why Emelina or I would want this investigation to continue?"

"She was your eyes and ears into the investigation. I shared with her everything the police told me. You knew how far we had gotten. Did you tell her to pull the plug after I told her that Murphy had an arrest warrant out on him for sexual assault?"

"Have you known anyone who ever told Emelina Bidwell what to do?"

"So, you are saying nothing good would come from you meeting with Detective Shafer?" Erin asks.

"I don't see an upside," he replies.

"What about pinning the murders on Johnny Murphy? Just last night you were happy to hear that the cases were solved, even though you knew the truth."

"And your point, Mrs. Strong?"

"Johnny Murphy may have done some really bad things, but it doesn't mean he did these bad things." I flip through the photos on my phone of the skeletons in front of him. "It's easy to pin this on a guy whose family was shamed out of town. You were willing to let that happen?"

He doesn't say anything.

"Sorry, Benjamin. A wise person once told me your reputation is the only thing you take to your grave." I don't bother to tell him that Johnny Murphy was in jail when Antoinette went missing. The case against Murphy will unravel once we do the show and tell with Shafer. The photographs on the desk are back in my daughter's possession. "Are you coming?"

He shakes his head.

We get up, then go down the hall to the entrance way and smile at the receptionist as we put on our hats, coats, and mittens. Outside, the temperature has dropped even more. It will be dark soon, and there is no way we are driving to the barracks in a raging snowstorm. I will ask the good detective to meet us at my house.

CHAPTER THIRTY-ONE

The water is calm, and it's the color of turquoise. Cruise ships pass by in the distance. My half-sister Brenda hooked us up with the best five-star hotel on Kingston's nicest beach. The people here couldn't be nicer. My children, along with Darren, my son-in-law, are frolicking in the water with my adorable grandchildren. Ken is sitting next to me on a beach chair and is resting his eyes. He only snores occasionally. The sun feels warm on my skin, the water cool on my toes.

Every dinner is at a different family member's house. I am getting to know my extended family from my birth mother's side.

We flew first class, as I had hoped, with a little assistance from Diane Rosenthal.

Abe and Emelina are taking turns watching Billy. After the Chamber party, we had cookie orders to fill for two solid weeks and finally caught a breather in time for us to take this trip in the second week of March. Another blizzard is pounding Milford as we enjoy Jamaica. I smile at our good fortune. I worry about those poor robins who venture north in February.

There are no more secrets between Emelina and me. Sworn to secrecy by Antoinette, Andrew, and Benjamin, she felt the only option was to use Johnny Murphy as a scapegoat. Given what she went through, how can I stay mad at her?

She has gone viral on TikTok, thanks to Erin, who manages our social media. Who doesn't love a centenarian giving out fifteen-second baking tips? Saturdays will be Chocolate Chip Cookie baking day, and all profits from sales will be donated equally between Milford's battered woman's shelter and its two soup kitchens.

When asked for his fingerprints, Benjamin Bloodstone lawyered up, but quickly cooperated. I didn't know that Shafer was able to obtain usable prints from the trunk Ken found in the basement. Maybe he did find prints or maybe he didn't. Shafer won't tell me, but it was enough to get Benjamin to talk.

Truscott Daniels and Mike Meade howled when Shafer served a search warrant on the Bloodstone Museum. A similar steamer trunk hidden away in the basement yielded Italian drapery and horsehair matching that found in the Devlin mansion steamer trunk. Horse racing records at Saratoga back in the 1920s showed that horses owned by Benjamin's grandfather raced there.

Mayor Scudder didn't put up a stink when Shafer legally seized Kenrick's revolver out of the display case in Borough Hall. Test firings proved the gun fired the fatal bullet that killed Andrew Bidwell.

The oil burner in the Devlin Mansion basement was traced to a supplier who sold it to A-1 Oil Delivery, owned by Chief Kenrick's brother. The niggling question of how the partition went up was now solved. Yes, the supplier had records going back fifty years. Something to do with retaining records for insurance purposes in case of product defect claims.

Ken was reinstated on the mansion restoration project, thanks to the owner's heartfelt apology and a higher budget.

Attorney Diane Rosenthal, who let us use her CaseSoft license, threatened to sue the Bloodstone Family Trust and the

Borough of Milford for the civil rights violations of the Bidwells. She brokered a deal, for a nice commission, in which Emelina would not file her suit in exchange for the Trust putting an endowment together to fund a new senior daycare center overlooking the river and named after Antoinette Bidwell, on land donated by the Borough and seized for back taxes. Everyone wants to call it a win-win-win. They come out smelling like roses, Milford's growing senior population gets a place to gather, and Emelina makes a lasting memorial to her niece.

Based upon Benjamin's admission of being the father of Antoinette's baby and the physical evidence, a strong circumstantial case is being made against Burgess Bloodstone and Herman Kenrick in the murders of Antoinette and Andrew Bidwell respectively. Shafer will let me know when the press conference will take place. He and Barney Williams will take equal credit. They didn't sweep any wrongdoings from fifty years ago under the rug. Accusing dead men of the crimes will close the cases, and Milford will eventually return to normal.

Colleen Flaherty had her baby, a boy, and took her family leave. As expected, I was not offered the opportunity to substitute. I would have turned the offer down anyway. I am too busy sleuthing and baking.

April interrupts my musing when she runs up to me from the water and says, "Grammy Strong, come in the water and give me a ride on your back." How can say I say no? I scoop her up in my arms. Life is too short, as I am constantly reminded.

"Whee!" April gleefully cries.

"Whee!" her seahorse repeats.

The End

Want more Gwen? One of Emelina's cookies is used as a murder weapon at the Milford Daffy Day Festival. The elderly woman is saved in the nick of time, but tells Gwen this is not the first attempt on her life. click here to start following the cookie crumbs Milford Daffy Day

ALSO BY J A HODA

Gwen's companion Billy appears in Milford Coal & Ice for the first time. As it asks on the bumper sticker *who rescued who?* Billy and Gwen must rescue a prize-winning show dog in a blizzard as nightfall is closing in. Download Milford Animal Rescue https://BookHip.com/BFXTNMT for FREE to your email inbox and join my newsletters for all thing Gwen

Want to start at the beginning?

Milford Elementary is book one in the Gwendolyn Strong Small Town Cozy Mystery Series

Everything Gwendolyn Strong learned about solving mysteries, she learned in kindergarten

One deceased groom-to-be. One dead-end clue. One last chance at redemption.

Gwendolyn Strong feels lost outside the classroom. And at loose ends after retiring, the ex-kindergarten teacher longs for the excitement her stable marriage and yoga sessions can't provide. So the spirited fifty-something leaps into action when a former student takes his life on the eve of his wedding day.

Skeptical that he died by his own hand, Gwendolyn teams up with her elderly mentor and true-crime addict daughter to scour the small town for clues while dodging the dismissive cops. But when her prime suspect turns up fatally crushed in a freak accident, she fears a cunning culprit could be pulling some murderous strings…

Can Gwendolyn solve the case before her name is next on the hit list?

Milford Elementary is the nail-biting first book in the Gwendolyn Strong Small Town Cozy Mystery Series. If you like whip-smart heroines, buried secrets, and gripping suspense, then you'll love J A Hoda's masterful whodunit.

Buy *Milford Elementary* (Book one) to send a killer to permanent time-out today!

Sift out the clues with Gwen. A nut allergy almost turns deadly at Milford's daffodil festival. When former kindergarten teacher Gwendolyn Strong starts delving into the elderly woman's claim that someone is trying to kill her, little does she realize that the killer won't stop until they get what they are after. Is it revenge? Is it money? Things get deadly serious when they make an attempt on Gwen's life. Does Gwen have the courage to continue sleuthing? Will she be able to be able to figure out who it is before they strike again?

Buy *Milford Daffy Day* (Book three) and follow along with Gwen as she finds more ingredients of this killer's deadly recipe. Milford Daffy Day

Coming December 19th, 2022

No way in. No way out. Who killed the party host? Follow the clues with Gwen in this present-day homage to locked room mysteries of the Golden Era in Milford Bed & Breakfast, book four in the Gwendolyn Strong Small Town Cozy Mystery Series

Gwendolyn Strong is invited to a sumptuous dinner. The occasion is the grand opening of a restored Victorian mansion overlooking the town as a bed and breakfast. Gwen's husband Ken performed the restoration. A wealthy stockbroker and his socialite wife invites their family, close friends, business associates and a glamorous movie star. In the morning, the host is found dead, shot in the head. This locked room whodunnit pays homage to Agatha Christie and John Dickson Carr. Can Gwen solve his murder? Phone lines are down and the only bridge to the mansion is washed away. The house is cut-off from outside assistance. Can Gwen solve the murder with just what she learned?

Buy *Milford Bed & Breakfast* (Book four) and race Gwen to the final reveal.

ACKNOWLEDGMENTS

Dave Pasquantonio for holding my hand during all edits and revisions.

Ruth Koizim for the extra set of eyes on the proofreading.

100 Covers for getting the covers perfect.

Susan Krauss, Pamela Tournier, Ilona Schmidt and the Fairfield Scribes for the deep dive critiques and encouragement.

ABOUT THE AUTHOR

J A Hoda graduated in 1975 with a B.S. in Criminology from Indiana University of Pennsylvania.

Hoda is a former Police Officer, Insurance Fraud Investigator and for the last 25 years has run a successful Private Investigations business. Many of his cases have made the headlines of the Philadelphia Inquirer and the New Haven Register.

He sat on the boards of the both the National Association of Legal Investigators and the CT Assoc. of Licensed Private Investigators. John is a Certified Legal Investigator and a Certified Fraud Examiner, retired.

He was feted as a debut novelist, panelist, and judge for the Shamus awards at the Mystery Writers of America Dallas Conference in 2019 with his first in the six-book FBI Agent Marsha O'Shea Series. Hoda produced and hosts a weekly podcast: My Favorite Detective Stories at www.johnhoda.com where he interviews crime fiction writers about their flawed fictional detectives.

He has won publisher awards for articles in The Legal Investigator and has written numerous articles for PI Magazine and other publications. He created the DVD: The Ultimate Guide to Taking Statements. He is a frequent guest blogger and webinar presenter on Investigative Interviewing. He has written four how-to books about the business side of private investigations and coaches PIs how to survive and thrive at www.ThePICoach.com

John answered the writing muse in 2013 with his debut novel: Second Chance at Bat. An average Joe though luck and circumstance gets a one in a million chance to play in the Major Leagues.

Through the years, Hoda told stories about his latest cases over coffee, at parties or at dinner engagements. Asked repeatedly to write them down, he finally did with: Mugshots: My Favorite Detective Stories

He was feted as a debut novelist, panelist, and judge for the Shamus awards at the Mystery Writers of America Dallas Conference in 2019 with his first in the six-book FBI Agent Marsha O'Shea Series.

John has been a lifetime athlete, playing club soccer and semi-professional football, running marathons, and bicycling long distance.

His other creative activities include stand-up storytelling and writing, producing, and acting in amateur theater.

He can be reached through his website https://jahoda.mailerpage.com or hodagen@gmail.com

Printed in the USA
CPSIA information can be obtained
at www.ICGtesting.com
LVHW040737220124
769331LV00044B/628